... T SERIES

THE COLDEST MOON

BY CHANEL HARDY

Printed in the United States of America.

Hardy Publications

chardypublications.com

This is a work of fiction. Any names or characters, businesses, events or incidents, are fictitious. Any resemblance to actual persons, living or dead, or actual events is purely coincidental.

New to the series?

Visit Amazon.com to purchase the first installment of the Moonlight Series, 'River's Moonlight'

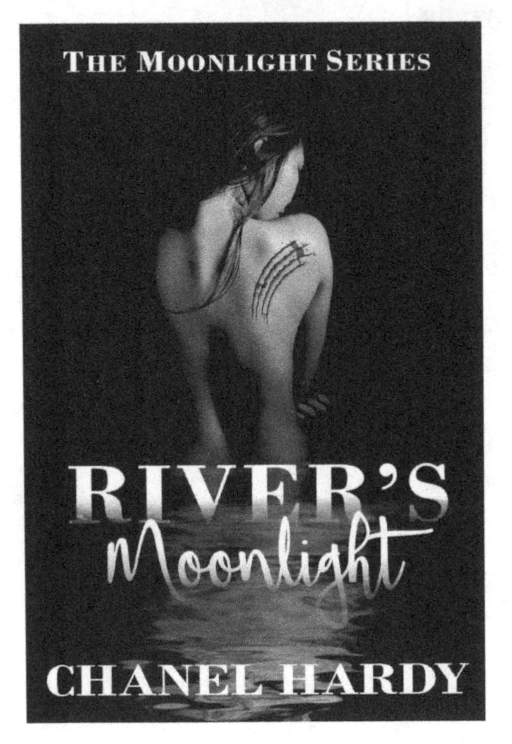

"Second chances don't always mean a happy ending.
Sometimes, it's just another shot to end things right."
-Unknown

CHAPTER 1

"We have to get far away from here and we need to go fast," said Jax.

He led River through the woods, pulling her forward as she tried to keep his pace. They had been walking for ten minutes already, and River's feet were becoming sore.

River stopped walking, leaning up against a tree to catch her breath. "I can't…I need to take a break." Her heart was thumping against her chest, and every bit of unfamiliar noise sounded like someone following behind them.

"It's all right. You can relax because there's no one behind us. We have time." Jax held her shoulder as she slouched down against the tree bark. "Give me the gun." He held out his hand, but River hesitated. "River, give it to me, please." He held a darting gaze.

Still gasping to catch her breath, she dug into the front of her pants and retrieved the pistol. With trembling hands, she placed it into his palm. Jax placed the gun in the back of his pants and pulled

River to her feet. They continued their run to the edge of the woods.

"Where are we going and what do we do now?" asked River breathlessly. She felt a tightness in her chest, panic rising from the unknown.

"We're going to my cabin. It's the only place we can go, for now. You'll be safe until I can figure all of this out. I promise."

"I need to go home, Jax. I want to go home. My aunt will be–"

"You can't go home." Jax came to a halt. "It's not safe."

"If it's not safe for me, it's not safe for her." River tugged on his arm, pleading for him to hear her out.

"So, what are you suggesting, River?" Jax gritted his teeth. "You want to tell her everything, including your transformation and the murder?" He stood facing her and clenching both her shoulders tightly. "I know you're worried about your aunt, but you need to listen to me. Shit is about to hit the fan and I need you to have your head on straight."

The look in his eyes was menacing, and the fear of what was in store for them hung from his face. River didn't know what to think. She felt terrified as if her life was rapidly ticking away as every second passed. With the death of Kayla on her hands, she knew her days were numbered. Days. More like hours if she was lucky. She knew that Jax would do whatever it took to keep her safe, but he wasn't untouchable. Her fate was sealed, and it would only be a matter of time before she paid for her crimes.

"I'll go with you," she said. "I'll do whatever I need to do. But I have to go home first. To say goodbye. You can't deny me that.

"Okay, but you can only stay for a minute, all right?" He brushed her cheek with his thumb.

"Okay." She held onto his hand, trusting him as a guide and a protector.

∞∞∞

River and Jax approached the gate to River's house. They checked their surroundings as they went to the front door. River's aunt Tasha had her car parked in her usual spot out front. A part of River hoped Tasha wouldn't be home, sparing her the heartache of saying goodbye, without an explanation as to why, or where she was going. River reached for the doorknob as a million thoughts of what to say ran through her head. She opened the door, flicking on the living room light on the wall to her right. Jax walked in beside her.

"Remember, only a minute," he whispered.

"I know. I won't be long." River was annoyed by his impatience. She understood that their situation was dire, but she expected more sympathy from him. A light turned on upstairs, and a shadow followed. Tasha approached the staircase, observing Jax and River. Jax quickly tossed Tasha's gun inside the fig tree that sat by the door, before she could notice.

Tasha glanced at the clock on the wall to her left. "Back already?" She walked down the stairs. "It's not even eleven o'clock yet." She peered in Jax's direction. "Nice to see you, Jackson."

"Likewise." He replied.

"Aunt Tasha…" said River as her voice trailed off. Her eyes became glossy as she mustered up the courage to speak.

"You all right?" Tasha squinted her eyes at River, picking up on her odd behavior. "Are you drunk? She placed her hand under River's chin and checked her pupils for signs of intoxication. "You look like you've had a rough night."

"I'm not drunk." River pushed Tasha's hand away. "It's not that…" Her lips began to quiver. Tasha's cop instincts were kicking in, and she knew something was up.

"What's going on? Did something happen at the party?" Tasha looked over at Jax, who avoided eye contact. She looked back at River. "Tell me, what's wrong?" River's emotions flooded the surface as her eyes welled up with tears. She didn't know where to start, or what to say.

"River, we don't have time," Jax said urgently. "We have to go soon."

Tasha's eyes widened. "River, what is he talking about?" River stood there, transfixed by the unsettling look in her aunt's eyes. "River, answer me!" Tasha was becoming frustrated as she began to raise her voice. River opened her mouth and tried to talk, but nothing came out.

Suddenly, a loud crash came from the kitchen, startling all three of them. The sounds of the heavy door hitting the floor vibrated beneath their feet. Tasha pushed River behind her, sticking her neck out toward the kitchen. She reached underneath her robe, grabbing her gun from her belt.

"Both of you go upstairs now," Tasha whispered. She held up her gun ready to face off with whoever, or whatever had made its way inside.

River and Jax shared a mutual glance, confirming they knew what was happening.

"We're not leaving you." River stood firmly behind Tasha.

"Dammit, River, go!" Tasha's clenched her teeth, and a vein emerged on her forehead. But it was too late. Multiple footsteps crept toward them. There was more than one person in the house. Jax sensed them before their figures emerged from around the corner.

"Leon." Jax felt a knot form in his stomach as he watched Leon and Desiree walk into the living room. Leon's face was cold, and sinister as he got closer. Jax didn't want things to end this way, but he knew that this standoff would only have one outcome. Someone was going to die.

Leon cracked his neck, rolling it side to side. "Looks like we've got the whole family here tonight, which makes it even better." His eyes were set on River, and he was ready for bloodshed.

Tasha pointed her gun with perfect aim. "Stay right there! Come any closer and I'll shoot!"

"Is that all you humans know how to do? Shoot guns? You're all weak and pathetic!" Leon's teeth began to shift, the sharp fangs of the beast emerging through as he spoke. Desiree stood close by, ready to strike with every passing second.

"Leon, please. This isn't the way." Jax slowly began to move in toward Leon, taking charge of the situation while he still had a few moments to spare. "Is this really how you want this to go down? You already lost one sister. Do you want to jeopardize the life of another?" Jax was breathing heavily, trying to put them at ease while having his guard up, preparing for Leon or Desiree to attack at any moment. River watched from behind Tasha, clenching on to the sleeve of her shirt, as the tension in the room heightened. She glanced at Desiree, whose eyes seemed empty. She looked hollow, like an empty shell of herself standing next to her brother.

Tasha tightened her grip on her gun, making River wince. "I don't know what's going on here, but you've got five seconds to leave this house before I shoot you both." She cocked her gun. "Five... four..."

"Desiree, if you do this, you'll have to face the council! Is this what you want?" Jax pleaded. His attempt at talking sense into her was pointless. She was too far gone. "Leon, you're making a mistake." Jax began to sweat, there was no turning back now.

Leon scoffed. "The only mistake I made was not killing you both when I had the chance. But you'll all be dying tonight." Leon's skin began to retract as the beast emerged, standing before them growling aggressively with bared teeth.

Tasha stood paralyzed in fear at what had taken place. Her hands trembled as she held onto the gun, trying not to lose her grip. Suddenly, Desiree transformed and charged toward Tasha. She fired three shots, and each one pierced Desiree's brute skull. Desiree dropped to the floor only a few inches from Tasha and River.

River recoiled as blood splattered on her face, but Tasha didn't move. She watched in horror as Leon attacked Tasha, slicing down her throat to her chest.

Images from the night at Lulu's flashed before River's eyes. Her vision blurred as her surroundings turned red. All she saw was blood. Jax had gone into full beast mode, going for Leon's neck, biting down, hard on his flesh. Leon yelped and shook him off vigorously, which sent Jax flying across the room.

River knew she needed to act quickly. While Leon was distracted, she remembered Jax tossed Tasha's other gun inside the fig tree. She dashed to the door, grabbed the gun, and aimed. She couldn't miss. Her and Jax's lives depended on it.

Leon focused his attention on River. He growled as his lucid eyes pointed straight to her. She faced him with her eyes widened, terrified to the core. She fired the gun in two, loud shots: one in his head and one in his chest. Leon whimpered and fell dead, smashing into the nearby glass table, shattering it to pieces. Jax immediately shifted back into human form and ran to River, who was limping out of breath. River gazed at Tasha, who lied in a pool of her own blood. Tasha was still breathing. River kneeled to comfort her.

"Aunt Tasha, please stay with me!" cried River. She pressed her hands over Tasha's wounds, but even she knew there was nothing she could do.

Tasha gagged for air as her mouth filled with blood. "My keys are…upstairs.

River shook her head. "I don't understand."

"My keys are…on the bed. Check my…purse." Tasha struggled to get the words out. "Take my car, the Nissan." Jax acted immediately, running upstairs to grab the car keys.

"I'm not leaving you! I'm calling an ambulance!" River's tears dripped onto Tasha's bloody face.

"It's too late for me. You need to go." Tasha slowly lowered her eyelids. "I love you. Take c-care of yourself, okay?" Tasha reached up to grab River's face with the last bit of energy she had left. Jax came bolting down the stairs, with Tasha's keys in hand.

He kneeled next to River, yanking her away. "I'm so sorry, but we have to go now."

"I can't!" River yelled in protest. Tears soaked River's face and bloodstained clothes as her aunt let out her last breath. Jax lifted River by her waist, dragging her from Tasha until they were outside.

Jax pressed the unlock button on Tasha's car key ring. He guided River into the passenger's side and then he slid around the roof of the car to the driver's side. Once the keys were in the ignition, he pulled off as the sounds of police sirens wailed in the distance.

CHAPTER 2

Hank had sensed that his children were in trouble, following their scent which led him to River's house. There were cop cars scattered all around the house. Lights flashing as people stood around nearby to see what was going on. He couldn't get inside, but the moment he could no longer sense Desiree and Leon, that's when he knew. His children were gone.

Rage filled him as he maintained his composure, blending in with the on-lookers outside. He watched as the paramedics carried out body after body. All three covered in white sheets. He knew two of them were his children. But he couldn't tell right away who the third victim was. He turned to a woman standing next to him, to try and get any info he could. "What happened in there?" He asked, trying to sound like a random nosey passerby.

"A home invasion I heard. Two kids dead, and a woman. She was a cop too."

A cop? Hank had no idea that River was affiliated with law enforcement. This increased his rage even more, as he clenched his right fist. He knew exactly what went down, despite any story law enforcement fed to the media. "Was anyone else hurt?"

"I don't know. But the cop's niece is missing. They don't know if she's involved yet." The woman stood with her arms crossed, sticking her neck out trying to get a better look at the bodies as they were carried out and placed in the back of the ambulance. Hank turned around, elbowing past a few people to get away from the crowd. He breathed in slowly, then out slowly. There was no time to mourn. He needed to get ahold of the council, and quick. Within two hours they were all gathered around Hank's table, waiting to get to the bottom of that night's disastrous events.

∞∞∞

River pressed her forehead against the cold window as they cruised down the highway. Raindrops trickled down the glass, as they both rode in silence. Jax clenched the wheel with both hands, staring straight ahead. River didn't even ask where they were going. It didn't matter. There was nowhere they could possibly run. A dead cop, three dead purebreds. Life was over for River as she knew it. If the cops didn't find her first, the council would. She could die in jail, or die at the hands of the shifter community. Those were her only options.

But Jax seemed caught in the middle of it all. She turned her head, watching him as he drove. She knew he didn't deserve this, and she couldn't allow him to go down with her. Enough people had suffered already. They took the next exit, pulling into a remote gas station that was about a mile ahead.

"We need to ditch the car." Jax parked at the edge of the parking lot, pulling the keys out of the ignition.

"What?" River tilted her head. "Do you think that's a good idea?"

"The police will be searching for you. They've probably already noticed that your aunt's car is missing too. We won't get far unless we ditch it. Now is our chance." There were three other vehicles parked at the gas station. Two at pumps, and one parked in front of the convince store. Jax scoped out their surroundings while River just stared at him.

"Are you crazy? I'm not doing this." She protested. River looked out of her passenger side window to see if anyone was watching them.

"We don't have a choice."

"We do have a choice. We could stop running. What difference will it make?"

Jax tapped the steering wheel with his thumbs. "No. I'm going to get you out of here" He wasn't determined to give up. River shook her head. There was no point in running. All Jax was doing was delaying the inevitable. It was exhausting, and River was tired.

"You should've just left me there. After I killed Kayla. You don't deserve this."

"I couldn't leave you. I didn't then, and I won't now." He reached over for River's arm, but she yanked it away. She opened her door and got out, slamming the door shut behind her. She leaned up against the car door in the pouring rain.

Jax got out and ran over to her. He stood facing her, resting his fingertips on the sides of her face as they both got soaked from the rain. She pulled his hands away, but Jax still held her hands as they dropped to her sides.

"You should just go." River pleaded. "I can't drag you down with me." River wanted him to save himself while he still had the chance.

"I can't leave you." Jax's voice grew softer.

"Why are you doing this?!"

Jax let go of her. "Because I love you!"

Hearing those words pour from his lips sparked something inside her. River didn't know how to respond. She wanted to say something, anything. But she had no words. This guy who had come into her life unexpectedly, was putting it all on the line, for her. His community, his life, all for love. She watched him as he stood there, longingly.

With a slumped posture, and her chin trembling, "I'm not worth it Jax."

"Yes you are." He seized her by the wrists, pulling her against him. She buried her face into his chest.

"I wish I could make it all just go away."

"I'll die before I let anyone hurt you." He wrapped both arms around her. "We'll get through this together. This isn't the end. I promise."

He looked back toward the convenience store, where there were two cars now parked. But it was too close in view of the store window. Suddenly, a car pulled up to one of the pumps. A middle-aged man got out of a pick-up truck. The engine was still running. Jax knew they had to go for it while the man went inside to pay for gas.

He watched as the man approached the store. "Come on, this way." He guided River toward the truck, ducking to avoid being spotted as they reached the driver's side door. He opened the door, helping River inside. She scooted over to the passenger seat. Jax hopped in right behind her. Turning the keys that were left in the ignition and flooring it out of there. River ducked as they sped away, peeking behind them to see if the man had come running when he heard his tires screeching. She couldn't see, but she imagined him standing with a beet red face, shouting obscenities.

She felt bad, but knew they had no choice. Jax was right about the police department being on the lookout for Tasha's car, and for River. Suspect or not, she was a minor on the run, with a dead officer and two dead strangers lying on the floor of her home. It would only be a matter of time before she became the top news story in Chicago. A feeling of relief rushed over River, as they managed to get far enough away from the gas station. She couldn't even see it in the distance. She scooted closer to Jax, resting her head on his shoulder while he drove.

"Where are we going?" She asked, watching the dark road ahead of them.

"Iowa." Jax said firmly. "I have a friend there who can help us."

ooooo

Hank lit the cigar that hung from his lips. A huge smoke cloud formed as he sat at the far end of his dining room table. To his left, sat Jon and Kareem. Across from them, Edward and Lester. Together, the four members formed the council in Region Two.

The elders were a large group of purebred shifters under the council, mostly over the age of fifty who helped maintain the values of the community. Like Hank, elders were hand-picked by the council members, as overseers to keep their region in check. The North American council consisted of three regions: West Region One, East Region Two, and South Region Three. The members of the council received their status by birthright. Holding the highest ranks from generation to generation. They were the judges, the jurors and the prosecutors.

"The boy. He's with her, isn't he?" Kareem sat with his hands folded, looking to Hank and patiently awaiting his answer.

"I'd assume they're halfway across the state by now." Said Edward.

"I'd assume so." Said Hank, still blowing smoke out of his nose and mouth.

"My apologies about your children Hank. As a father, you have my condolences." Kareem cleared his throat, adjusting his tie. "But as a member of the community, I must express deep disappointment in you, and your children's poor choices that led to their demise. I expected better from your teachings." The rest of the council members nodded in agreement. "With that being said, we are revoking your title as an elder."

"You cannot be serious!" Hank smashed the edge his cigar into the ashtray next to him. "If we had infiltrated the police department years ago, none of this would be an issue!"

"Don't turn this around Hank. This isn't about the community, or how we choose to do things. This is about your poor parenting" Said Jon. Hank slammed his fist down on the table, leaving a slight crack in the glass. Jon's eyes bulged at Hank's aggression.

"Hank, calm yourself. I will not tolerate this behavior from you." Kareem glared at Hank, reminding him of who was in charge. "We've been trying to figure out what to do about the feys. They're getting out of control. Their existence puts us at risk more each day."

"What are you suggesting?" Hank asked in a huff, still angry at Jon's remark.

Lester chimed in. “An extermination.”

Hank’s eyebrow raised. This was serious. Not since the dawn of the shifter’s existence, had a plan to wipe out their own been constructed to this magnitude “What do the other regions have to say about this?” He asked.

“That will be discussed when the time comes.” Sad Kareem. First, we need to find the girl. Jackson too. It doesn’t matter where they run too. There is no escaping the council.” Kareem stood up from his chair. All except Hank followed suit. “We’ll start putting together a search. They should be found in no time. Proper punishment will be given.”

“We’ll be in touch.” Jon smirked before turning, to head out of the dining room followed by the others. Hank remained in his chair. Alone, wondering where it all went wrong. How it all came to this. He stared at the empty seats at the table, where the memories of his children lingered. He resisted the urge to get revenge on his own. The mourning of his kids was overshadowing his values and loyalty to the community. His eyes began to water, as one tear slid down his cheek. Hank had never cried before. His weakness was breaking through. He wiped away the single tear. River and Jax were going to pay.

CHAPTER 3

River laid with her arm stretched across Jax's torso. They were both nude, snuggled under the sheets of the motel bed. The rays from the sun beamed horizontally in through the blinds of the window, giving his skin a mellow glow.

After driving for two hours in the middle of the night, they made it to Rockford. They stopped at a local Shop Mart to pick up a change of clothes, and got a room at a motel in a small town a few miles off the highway. Jax stopped at a bank once they got to Rockford, withdrawing all of the money he had left in cash.

River ran her finger's over his bare chest, feeling his heart beating underneath his sternum while he slept. He felt warm. He looked so peaceful, and for the first time in weeks, River felt safe. Even if the feeling was short-lived.

"I didn't know you could drive." She said softly. Jax stirred lightly in his sleep.

"What did you say?" He mumbled under his breath, as he moved his head, with his eyes still closed.

"I didn't know you could drive. You're good at it."

Jax rubbed his eyes, tilting his head to look down at her. "There's a lot you don't know about me." He cracked a smile, kissing her forehead. "I may have lived in the woods, but I wasn't entirely useless. Growing up with Hank actually had its benefits." Hearing Hank's name out loud made River's stomach drop.

"What happens when they find us?" River peered up at him. He lifted her arm, sitting up with his back against the bed frame. He was quiet, his face dejected. River sat up with him, holding the blanket over her breasts. "Jax, please say something."

Jax's eyes were stretched forward, studying the wall from across the room. He lifted the covers off himself, turning to sit on the side of the bed. His elbows sat on his thighs, as he dropped his head, looking down to the floor. He dreaded this conversation, but it was time that River knew the grisly truth about the council. The horrifying fate of those who broke the rules, and how this shaped his entire existence.

"I was ten when Hank was sworn in as an elder. He took Kayla, Leon, Desiree and I to Jefferson City in Missouri. There was a purebred being executed for killing a family of humans staying at a lake house one night." Jax ran his fingers over his mouth. "Hank he… wanted us to watch." River clasped her hands over her mouth, as she listened to Jax's detailed accounts of witnessing his first murder. "Hank wanted us to see the gravity of the consequences with our own eyes. What would happen if we went against the code. If we killed." Jax's hands started to tremble as he circled his thumbs. "They hung the man upside down, his ankles were tied with rope. His hands too. I still remember the look in his eyes. He looked right at me." Jax's voice cracked as he recalled the man's face in his memory. "They poured gasoline all over him, then a council member lit the torch." Jax's eyes began to well up, tears slid down his face and on to his lap.

River's sat with her mouth gaped open. Immobilized by the fear of being burned alive. In all the ways she imagined her death, being set ablaze was not one of them. It was barbaric. "How can they do that? It's insane." Now it made sense, why Jax had this perpetual need to help feys. After witnessing such a harrowing death, he made sure that those who were cursed could maintain their lives with the beast inside of them, like purebreds could.

"When they were finished, there was nothing left but a small lump of charred flesh. I didn't sleep for days afterwards." Jax wiped his face, and turned River.

"I'm so sorry. I can't even imagine." River placed her hand on his back.

"I'm not going to let that happen to you. Or to me, you got that?" He slid around, clutching River's jaw with both hands. He pulled himself closer to her, pressing his forehead against hers. "When we get to Iowa, there's a town called Bertram. They won't be able to find us there. We'll be safe. Don't you worry." He nuzzled her nose, before pressing his lip against hers. "If we leave now, we can make it there by noon." His thumb traced the lines of her jaw. She shook her head, conceding his plan. She was ready to go wherever Jax was ready to take her.

∞∞∞

Kareem swiped through the holographic screen that projected on to the round, onyx marble table in the middle of headquarters. His index finger scrolled through photos of River. He swiped to a photo of Jax then back to River, pursing his lips. Altogether, Jax appeared in two photos. One of him at ten years old, and the other more recent, taken just two years ago. The photos of River were taken from her home, social media profiles and pulled from online news coverage about her attack at Lulu's and her disappearance. The council had information on every shifter that resided in their district. It didn't matter where you came from, or what type of lifestyle you lived. If you were pure or cursed, the council knew. The other members of the council sat spaced apart around the table, hands folded, and stone-faced waiting for Kareem to speak.

"One of our brothers spotted an abandoned car at a gas station off highway 67. It had the scent of a shifter." Kareem peered down at the photos again. "We believe they are in or around the Rockford area. The scent of the fey shouldn't be hard to pick up. It won't be long now." The council members wore identical expressions, their faces brooding, their wicked smiles, ominous "The girl will burn first, the boy can watch. We'll deal with him our own way. He needs a lesson, on what happens when you betray your pack for a fey."

While not forbidden, it was frowned upon for purebreds to mate with or have any romantic relationships with feys. It put their community's way of life at risk, and compromised their values. In particular, purebreds couldn't associate with humans unless it was necessary to sustain their everyday lives. Jax's father, Silas was one of the very few purebreds who had ever formed a relationship with a fey. Silas' love for Jax's mother Carla, ultimately led to his demise.

When Jax was a child, Hank told him that his father was killed by a human. That he was shot during a full moon, by a hunter in the woods. Jax never questioned it, as he had no reason to. He trusted Hank, and believed in his words. But that wasn't the truth. There was more to Jax's past, and more to the story of his parents passing than a simple case of doomed lovers.

"Will we ever tell him?" Asked Jon, from the left side of the circle. There was a moment of silence as Edward and Lester looked at him, then back at Kareem as they waited for his reply.

Kareem's face wore an evil grin. "No need to tell him anything. He won't be alive long enough for it to matter." He swiped the screen away completely, peering down at his own reflection on the table.

Chapter 4

Jax and River were nearing the state border, less than two hours away from Bertram. Jax pulled into a gas station to fill up for the final half of their drive to Iowa. River wore a navy-blue baseball cap, trying to mask her identity as best she could. She tossed the hood of her jacket over the hat. Stray strands from her fuzzy braids stuck out from underneath the hood. Jax went inside the mini mart to pay for gas, while River switched through radio stations, trying to find music to calm her nerves. Tasha had been on her mind all morning. A part of River still couldn't mentally process that her aunt was gone. She tried to remember her as she was. Her smile, the plum lipstick she always wore. The smell of her Blue Magic hair grease that River used to cringe at when she was a little girl. Simple things that River took for granted, she would never see, smell, or feel again. The dial landed on a station that was covering the news story of the murders. *A home invasion.* That's what the voice on the radio called it.

"Seventeen-year-old River Lewis, the niece of Detective Tasha Lewis who was murdered last night in their home, is still missing. There are no leads on her whereabouts as of yet. If you see anyone matching her description, please contact the local authorities immediately. Our thoughts and prayers are with the Chicago Police Department as they mourn the loss of a beloved officer."

River turned off the radio, she couldn't listen to anymore. Her heart started racing as her chest began to tighten. Her fingers, trembling as she rubbed them back and forth against her lap to ease her anxiety. It wasn't working. She saw Jax coming back toward the truck, reaching for the gas pump. She opened her passenger door, getting out to walk around to his side.

"What are you doing?" He asked her.

"I'm feeling a little light headed. I'm gonna go inside and grab a ginger ale." River rubbed the sides of her head. Jax didn't like the idea of her being out and exposed during the day. Even with a mild disguise.

"Just be quick." He figured a few minutes wouldn't hurt. River jogged over to the mini mart, walking through the door quickly with her head down avoiding eye contact with anyone around her. She walked past the counter, heading for the beverage coolers. As she opened the door to one of the coolers, a man reached inside, towering over her. She jumped, looking up at the man who had invaded her personal space.

"Sorry about that love." The man grabbed a bottle of water, his lips were raised slightly, as if he was trying to hold back a smile. River didn't respond. Her eyes just followed his as he leered at her, standing close enough to smell what she had for breakfast. His eyes were grey, and his dark hair was pulled back into a ponytail. Something about him gave River chills. He was dressed in all black, like he was headed to a funeral. He walked away, and River quickly grabbed her drink and sprinted toward the counter.

"Two dollars." The old man at the counter didn't even look up from his newspaper. River glanced at the paper he was reading, and there on the front page, was Tasha's photo. *Veteran Cop Killed in Home Invasion*. River's heart skipped a beat, and the tightness in her chest was coming back. In the upper right corner, was her own photo. *Teen Missing*. The man looked up from his paper. "Two dollars." He demanded again. Snapping back into reality, River fiddled through her pockets for lose bills. She then realized that she had spent it back at the motel vending machine.

"Never mind." She slid the soda toward the clerk. But before she could walk away, someone slammed a five-dollar bill on the counter. River looked to her right. It was the man again.

"It's on me." His lips actually formed a full smile this time. An eerie, unpleasant smile. River grabbed the soda and headed for the door, resisting the urge to look back at him. She could feel his eyes on her back as she power walked to the truck. Jax was already sitting inside waiting to pull off. River ran around to the passenger's side, hopping in with swiftness.

"You alright?" Jax asked with furrowed brows.

"Yeah. Let's just go." River didn't want to bring up the man in the mini mart. She couldn't shake the feeling that something was off about him. Their encounter left a sour feeling in her stomach. As Jax drove out the gas station, River turned around, checking to see if the man was watching. When she didn't see him, she silently blew a sigh of relief. She had a theory, but didn't want her paranoia getting the best of her. She knew she had to stay positive. It wouldn't be long before her and Jax made it to Bertram, and could finally let their guard down.

The trees began to resemble big green blurs as they drove down a long stretch of road, with only a few cars up ahead. They were finally far enough away from the city, where everything became unfamiliar. River didn't know what to expect when they arrived to Bertram. Jax told her that it was a small town, with a population of less than three hundred people.

She knew that they would be meeting someone there, a friend of Jax. He didn't go into too much detail about this friend, but River didn't bother to ask. She assumed this person was a shifter. Jax didn't know any regular humans. Not to her knowledge at least. It didn't matter either way. If Jax vouched for him and he could guarantee their safety, then River wasn't going to ask a million questions. Getting out of Illinois was all she cared about right now.

"Don't be scared, but I think that black car has been following us." Jax kept his eyes on the road, trying to remain calm. River's eyes widened, she looked at Jax, then snapped her head around to see the car that he was referring too. It's windows were tinted, and the car kept a distance to avoid suspicion. "I noticed them about fifteen minutes ago. I didn't think anything of it at first, but when we started turning, so did they." Jax peered into the rearview mirror. "It can't be a coincidence." River's heart started to pound heavily as her fears were becoming a reality.

Jax was right, this couldn't have been a coincidence. River thought about the man with the ponytail at the mini mart. She prayed that she was wrong about him, and began to regret not bringing him up to Jax earlier.

The black car picked up speed, and so did Jax. They caught up to the truck, slowing down to get a good look. The black car picked up speed again, getting ahead of the truck, before swerving over to the right, cutting them off and coming to a complete stop. Jax slammed on the breaks, sending him and River jerking forwards. Jax clenched the wheel dreading what was about to unfold. River's breathing increased, her palms felt sweaty.

"Oh my god." River grabbed his arm, hoping he had a plan to get them out of this. "What do we do now?" she asked franticly. But Jax just sat there, unresponsive, staring forward, his hands still clutching the wheel. That's when River knew. It was all over. Both the driver's and passenger doors opened in unison as two men got out. Chills ran through River when she noticed the driver. It was him. The man from the mini mart. "We've gotta go! We've gotta run! Now!" She shook Jax's arm, not understanding why he wasn't moving. "Jax, please!"

"It's going to be okay." His voice was calm. He looked over at River, who was panicking with tears in her eyes.

"I'm sorry, I can't." River opened the door, bolting for the woods. She was too late, as the ponytail man caught her before she could get away. River kicked and screamed, flailing her legs around trying to escape his grip.

"Let go of her! Please! Just take me!" Jax begged as the second man yanked him out of the driver's side seat, dragging him over to the car.

"Stop fighting. It won't do you any good." The ponytail man said to River, as he dragged her over to the car, pushing her up against the vehicle, next to Jax. "I gotta say, we're shocked you got this far." He grinned at River. "But your little road trip is over." He reached into his jacket, pulling out a syringe filled with orange liquid. The second man did the same, holding an identical syringe up to Jax's neck.

Seeing the syringe ignited River's will to live. She clawed at his face, lodging her right index finger into the ponytail man's left eye. Her sharp nail, piercing his eyeball with all the strength she could muster. He dropped the syringe, shrieking out in pain as blood gushed from his eye. His accomplice became distracted, giving Jax the chance to take hold of the syringe in his hand, shoving the needle into the man's neck. He dropped to the ground, out cold. The ponytail man reached for River, yanking her by the collar and shoving her face-first onto the ground. Jax ran for the other syringe before the man could reach it, putting him in a headlock and shoving the syringe into his neck. Both men laid motionless in the middle of the street as Jax and River ran back to the truck. Jax's foot hit the accelerator so fast, River could see smoke emanate from the tires.

Jax kept driving until they reached the sign that read *Welcome to Bertram: population 286*. River hadn't spoken to Jax at all up until that point. He asked her if she was alright a few minutes after they escaped the council's henchmen, but she didn't say anything. She just nodded. They checked behind them every few minutes, making sure that nobody else was following them. Thankfully, they were in the clear.

Jax stopped the car, taking in a deep breath. He couldn't believe that they actually got away. If River hadn't done what she did, they'd be on their way to their deaths right now. River opened the door, jumping out and slamming it behind her. She ran toward the snow-covered grassy area next to the road, pacing in circles and burying her face in her hands.

Jax got out to go after her. "River, where are you going!?" He approached her, and she turned toward him, trembling. She pushed him, he stumbled backwards.

"I can't believe you!" She began to push him repeatedly. "You were just going to let them take us?!" Jax gripped her hands before she could push him a fourth time. "Let me go!"

"No!" Jax pulled her in close, trying to calm her down. "River, stop! I'm sorry alright!" River tried to yank her arms away, clenching her jaw. She didn't want to hear it. "I froze back there, and I shouldn't have. I should've fought harder to protect you. I let you down, I know." River's head dropped, she couldn't look at him. "I screwed up." He let her hands go. "But we made it, and that's all that matters now. I'm proud of you, for what you did back there." She looked up at him, pursing her lips with her arms folded. "You saved us. We made it because of you."

As much as she wanted to hate him for giving up, she couldn't. He had been strong for her all this time, and it wasn't fair for her to chastise him for being human. He had a weak moment, and it wasn't his fault.

"I was so scared Jax." She was still trembling as she tried to come down from her anxiety-ridden outburst.

"I was too." He got closer, slouching down and resting his head onto her shoulder. He wrapped his arms around her waist, For the first time since they met, River was witnessing him in a vulnerable state. He had spent so much time saving her, that it never crossed her mind that he needed saving too. She placed her hand on the back of his neck, his soft curls tickling in between her fingers. River explored the area surrounding them. The crisp air from the cold temps prickled her face. There was nothing in sight, but grass covered in patches of melting snow. The outline of houses were stretched out in the distance. It was serene. River rubbed her face against his head, his hair brushing up against her cheek.

She whispered softly near his ear. "We made it baby."

Chapter 5

River and Jax drove through Bertram, passing locals who peered into the truck occasionally. They were held up at a stop light, where a white woman was walking by along the sidewalk with a young boy. The little boy, who looked to be about five years old, just stared at River with his mouth hanging open. Drool dripped from his lips as he and River made eye contact. River smiled at him, but he didn't smile back. She looked at the woman he was with, who had noticed that something held the boy's attention. She glanced at River with narrow eyes, then yanked the boys arm so he could keep up.

"What did I tell you about staring?" She said to him. They continued along, but the boy kept looking back at the truck, bemused by River.

"I'm guessing Bertram isn't known for its diversity, huh?" River turned to Jax as he drove through the changing light.

"They're friendly people." Jax smiled, but River wasn't amused. Jax's racially ambiguous features allowed people like him to fit in anywhere. River on the other hand, couldn't escape her blackness even with her mother's Southeastern Asian features blended in.

"We'll I at least hope your friend is friendly." River said with a smirk.

"He is. His name is Will. He's a fey."

River was relieved to know that it wasn't a purebred. For the first time since her turn, she'd be around someone who was just like her. But she wondered how he was able to fly under the radar. If the council didn't know about him, then there had to be a reason why. "How do you know him?" She asked.

"A few years ago, when I first moved out on my own, I used to go to the library every day to look up news stories on strange animal attacks from all over the country. I could easily tell if it was a shifter attack based on specific details about the victims. If they survived, I'd search for them. To teach them how to live with it." River listened, captivated by his anecdotes of helping the cursed. "I've travelled all over. Some feys I've been able to help, and some, not so much." His tone went fragile, as memories of those he couldn't save flashed through his mind.

"But you saved Will?" River's eyes were focused on him. He breathed in and out slowly through his nose, running his tongue across his teeth. He didn't answer her question.

"We're here." Jax turned right on to a small path that looked like it led to a dead end. There was a "Road Closed" sign on the side of the path. *Smart guy*. River thought. The closer they got, the easier the house became to spot. It was a wide, two level structure. It's exterior was an eggshell white, with shutters hanging off at the hinges and chips in the paint that were visible from the car. Tall, unmanaged grass surrounded the house. Jax could've told her that the place was abandoned, and she would've believed him. Jax parked in front of the house, getting out to meet River on the passenger's side. He held her hand as she gazed at the house, with uncertainty in her eyes. As they walked up the porch, River got an eerie feeling about the house. Jax opened the screen door, knocking loudly. River looked around, and noticed a device with a small red dot in the upper left corner of the window. Jax knocked again.

"I think he knows we're here." River tugged at the arm of his jacket, pointing at the camera. Jax heard a soft click from behind. With his sharp reflexes, he grabbed River, jerking around and shoving her behind him. River didn't even have time to react to what was going on. Then she saw him, standing at the foot of the steps with a rifle pointed directly at them.

"Will, it's me. Don't shoot." Jax had his hands up, as River clung to him, her eyes wide and her heart racing. The barrel of the shotgun didn't budge. "Will, don't shoot please."

"Who is she?" Will's voice was deep, he sounded almost robotic.

"Her name is River. She's with me. She's a fey." Jax still had his hands up, hoping Will would listen to him. "We came here because we need your help."

Will lowered his gun, and began walking up the porch steps with the rifle at his side. He stood face to face with Jax, their eyes glued to each other. River didn't know what to expect. Will's long, thick dreadlocks hung down the sides of his face like rope. He had a scar on his cheek that expanded to his mouth. Jax said this guy was a friend, but right now it looked like the opposite.

"I almost killed you." Will said.

"Wouldn't be the first time." Jax smiled, and suddenly the tension was gone. Will's mouth formed a crooked grin, as he pulled Jax in for a hug, Jax welcomed him, and River could feel the bond they shared, radiating from their affection towards each other.

"Long time no see bro." Said Jax.

"Too long." Jax turned to River, who was still a bit shaken up from having a gun pointed at her. "This is River. We need your help. It's bad."

"Say no more. Let's get inside." Will moved past them to unlock the door. He pushed it open, stepping aside for them to come in. The house was dark, and there were large white sheets draped over furniture. Dust covered the floors, windows, anything where dust could possibly reach. "Follow me." He led them to a door, that led to the basement. The door creaked open as they followed Will downstairs. River scrunched her face, confused as she took each raggedy step down into the dark basement.

"What's down here?" She asked, as they reached the bottom. Will stood in the middle of the floor. "My sanctuary." He kneeled down, lifting up a big square shaped door that blended in with the dark floor tile. "Ladies first." River looked at him like he was crazy. She had no idea what was down there, and was hesitant to find out.

"It's alright. I'll be right behind you." Jax told her. She thought about the council, and knew that if she wanted to be safe, she had to do what was being asked, even if it seemed insane. She walked over, peeking down into the gaping hole. There was a ladder attached at the edge. She turned around, going in feet first. She scaled down the ladder, and underneath her feet, she could see a light. This eased her nerves as she looked above her, and could see Jax following her down. At the bottom, there was a hallway where the light illuminated. She waited for

Jax and Will to reach the bottom. Will led them down the small hallway, where there were three small rooms. River understood now. How Will was able to hide from the council.

"Shifters can't track your scent down here. It's where I spend most of my time." He led them to one of the rooms. "Are you sure they haven't followed you here?"

"I'm sure. For the last hour and a half of our trip, there weren't any consistent cars behind us. We kept track this time." Jax told him.

Will cocked his head, narrowing his eyes. "What do you mean, this time?" Jax and River looked at each other, then back at Will.

"You're going to want to sit down for this." Said Jax.

Chapter 6

Kareem ran his right index finger across the edge of the countertop as he slowly paced around Jax's kitchen. Jon, Lester and Edward ransacked the cabin, searching for any clues as to where Jax and River could be. After the two henchmen failed to capture them that morning, the council was outraged.

Both men were found passed out in the middle of the road by a passing driver after Jax and River had gotten away. They were still unconscious from the serum, so they were taken to a hospital where they awoke later. Once the men realized where they were, they left the hospital in a panic, contacting the council immediately to explain what had happened.

The council viewed the henchmen's incompetence as unacceptable. Both men were executed upon their arrival at headquarters. The council had no other leads and had to stoop to drastic measures to find Jax and River.

Kareem opened the cabinets where a few clean dishes sat neatly stacked. He was surprised that Jax kept the place so tidy. He was very well-ordered for someone who lived in the woods.

"Bingo." Lester called out from Jax's bedroom.

Kareem went to the bedroom to see what Lester found. In the room, Lester had slid the bed, flipped the mattress, and scattered clothes everywhere. He held a small shoebox in his left hand, with a bunch of papers in his right. Jon and Edward were standing next to him, and the three of them smiled menacingly. Kareem walked over to them, grabbing the papers from Lester's hand. He swapped through them one page at a time, trying to figure out the importance of the documents.

After thumbing through a few more pages, he discovered what it was. The papers included lists of names and addresses. The other pages featured printed out newspaper clippings and map directions. The document was information on all the feys that Jax had researched. The council knew of his travels in the past and dealings with feys, but they never monitored him closely. Kareem chuckled as he was amused that everything, they needed was conveniently laid out for them.

"Where did you find this?" Kareem asked.

"Hidden behind a small compartment behind the headboard, said Lester as he pointed to the disheveled bed. I almost missed it. He's a clever kid."

"Not clever enough." Kareem shoved the papers inside his blazer. "Let's get going. We don't have any more time to waste.

ꝏꝏꝏ

River tossed and turned on the queen-sized mattress that sat in the corner of the room. Jax slept behind her, with his hand stretched across her torso underneath the itchy, polyester blanket. River hadn't been able to sleep at all, flicking the switch on her flashlight. She pulled her hands inside her long sleeve shirt. Will had a portable electric heater that kept them warm as the temperature dropped into the thirties overnight.

She missed the snug warmth of the motel room back in Rockford. She wished they could've stayed there under the plush, white covers. Still, the sacrifice for safety at Will's house was worth it.

River wondered how long they'd have to stay at the house, hiding out like fugitives. Will's underground bunker was the perfect hiding spot, but River couldn't imagine her and Jax staying there forever. She pondered if staying alive would matter if it meant a life of seclusion. River rid her head of these thoughts.

She thought about Tasha, who would've wanted her to survive no matter what it cost. After they told Will about what happened at the party, the attack at River's house, and even Tatiana's death, he contemplated on making them leave. He felt as though River was a liability, and her irrational actions at the party put the lives of every fey in the country at risk. Jax pleaded with him to let them stay, even if it was only temporary. Will agreed, only because he loathed everything about the council and the shifter community and felt like he owed a debt to Jax.

River had been holding in the urge to pee, feeling uneasy about leaving the bunker in the middle of the night. She could feel her bladder filling, and the need to urinate trumped her fear of going upstairs alone. She gently pushed Jax's arm aside as she sat up, trying not to wake him. He flinched in his sleep, but he didn't wake. River got up, adjusting the blanket over him, before making her way to the ladder that led upstairs. She climbed up, unlatching the hook and pushing the door open.

Lifting herself into the bunker, she noticed the basement door slightly open. She and Jax slept in the first room, so River couldn't see if Will was sleeping when she left. She walked upstairs and heard footsteps against the creaking floorboards. Goosebumps appeared on her skin as she waited at the top of the steps, hiding behind the door.

A shadowy figure approached. Peeping through the crack of the door, she knew the mystery person was probably Will, but she didn't want to risk being seen in case it wasn't him. Suddenly, she saw Will, walking past the basement with something in his hands. He walked into another room, which seemed to be the kitchen based on River's memory of being upstairs earlier. She opened the door and headed in his direction. She heard fumbling sounds as she approached the kitchen where Will was sitting at a table. He had a bear trap in front of him, with a dead rabbit caught in its claws. As River approached the kitchen, the floorboard creaked and startled Will. He drew his pistol, and River gasped, stopping in her tracks. She threw her hands up.

"It's just me," she said quietly. Will let out a deep breath, lowering his weapon.

"You can't just sneak up on people like that," he huffed, placing his gun on the table. "What are you doing up here?"

"I was just coming to use the bathroom. I heard someone walking around." River put her hands down.

"Well, if it wasn't me, you'd be dead by now." Will rolled his eyes. "I guess stupid decisions are a common thing with you, huh?"

River furrowed her eyebrows. "Excuse me?"

Will shook his head, pulling the rabbit flesh from the trap. "I'm just being honest."

River's facial expression didn't change. "Honest? You don't even know me." She folded her arms, getting defensive.

"I know enough," said Will as he wiped the bear trap with a wet cloth, focusing on the task.

River was upset but she didn't want to start any trouble. She and Jax were guests in Will's home. She decided to disregard his rudeness and head to the bathroom.

"He really loves you," Will said.

Will's comment made River pause, and she turned to him. "Jackson has a heart of gold. That's how we became friends. But I'm sure you knew that." Will cracked a small smile, and River walked to the table, pulling out the metal chair to sit across from him. "I don't know where I'd be right now if Jax hadn't found me. He saved me in more ways than one."

"I had already killed two people when Jax found me," said Will as he put down the bear trap. "My last victim was a kid, an eight-year-old boy." Will pressed his lips, trying to hold back tears as he recalled the memory. "After that, I just couldn't do it anymore. I grabbed my gun and called my momma to tell her I loved her. Then, I put the pistol in my mouth and pulled the trigger."

River's eyes widened as she listened to his heartbreaking testimony. His story was beginning to sound a bit too familiar. She thought about the eight-year-old boy Will mentioned, and then everything became clear.

"It's you," she whispered. "You're midnightclaw." She remembered she had read his blog entries the day she turned for the first time.

Will stared at her. "You read my blog?"

River couldn't believe it was him, but it made sense. The location, the amount of time that Will and Jax have been friends. Jax told River that he met Will in 2014, and Will was the same age as the man from the blog based on the profile details.

Will chuckled. "I can't believe anyone actually read those or that I actually wrote that stuff."

River smiled. "Your posts helped me when I was in denial. I remember reading them and getting goosebumps. I thought to myself, this can't be real."

River stared blankly as she recollected the events of that fateful day. “I turned that same night. But the turn wasn’t the only thing that changed me.” River fiddled with the edges of her sleeves.

“Well, I’m no hero. I was just a troubled guy with nowhere else to turn.” Will got up from the table, walking over to the counter to grab a trash bag from the cabinet underneath the sink. “The night I tried to blow my brains out, was the night Jax found me. I missed the shot. Then, I was unconscious and woke up disfigured.” Will stood at the counter with his hands clenched and his head down. “Jax was following me that day. It’s a good thing that he was, or I would’ve bled out on that floor.” He turned around to face River. “He took me to the hospital, where I was pronounced dead not too long after. But they were wrong. I wasn’t dead. I got a second chance.”

River could tell the situation was difficult for him to discuss. River got up from the table and walked toward him. Will leaned his back against the counter, too ashamed to look River in the eyes as she came closer.

River stood in front of him. “I thought about it, too. Suicide.”, She raised her left hand to touch the scar on his face, but he caught her hand before she could reach him.

“Don’t do that.” Will’s nostrils flared as he breathed heavily, and his eyes pierced into hers. He grabbed the black garbage bag, stomped back to the table, and tossed the dead rabbit inside it.

“I didn’t mean to. It was rude. I’m sorr-”

“Don’t ever think about taking your own life.” Will continued. He walked back over to River, with the trash bag dangling from his side. “The healing process is ugly, River. Coming to terms with what we are? It’s shit. But it takes accountability, which brings guilt. It’s triggering, but processing trauma often means you have to relive it. It sucks, but it’s how we get through it. Being alive is always worth it.”

River stood there, allowing his words to resonate with her. She felt his pain, every ounce of it, and knew he could feel hers, too. After all, they were more alike than she and Jax could ever be. They were human beings thrown into a world of death, darkness, and torture. They had to abandon everything they had ever known to live this life. A life of the cursed.

Will placed his hand on River's shoulder. "Jax is like a brother to me. Whatever happened back in Chicago, it's in the past now. Just know that when the day comes, I'll be ready to fight whatever battle comes your way. If I'm going to die, I'm taking some purebreds with me."

CHAPTER 7

Theodora Banks

2232 Borders Ln #102

Alexandria, VA

The council and two of their henchmen approached the three-story apartment building at ten past midnight. They broke the lock on the front door and headed to the unit of 26-year-old Theodora Banks. She was the first on Jax's list, and the first fey to face the brutal interrogation of the council. Lester knocked once, making sure that he and the rest of them were in perfect view of the peep hole. Lester knocked again, and this time they could hear someone approaching.

"Who is it?" Theodora asked with a raspy voice.

"'Theodora Banks,' said Lester in a low, sinister voice, 'We have a few questions for you if you'd be so kind as to open the door.'"

She paused, frightened and unsure if she should answer. "Just a minute." Theodora ran to her bedroom to grab her gun from under her bed. She approached her door slowly, with the gun held up to her cheek. She unlocked the top lock, opening the door slightly, with the chain still attached. “Who are you?”

“We are the council.” Answered Lester.

She inhaled suddenly. Fear rushed through her as she realized what was going on. Pushing the door closed, one of the henchmen kicked it open, sending Theodora flying backwards. One of the henchmen pulled out a tranquilizer gun, and shot a dart laced with a sedative flying into her leg. Before her screams could reach the top of her throat, she was unconscious.

“Grab her now.” Kareem ordered the henchmen to take Theodora to the car quickly and quietly. They tossed her in the trunk of the black SUV, leaving the scene as discreetly as possible.

They took Theodora to a nearby wooded area, parking the car on the side of the road and leaving one henchman to be the lookout. They dragged her about a mile and a half deep into the woods, her arms and legs bound by thick rope and her mouth duct taped. Lester tossed a bucket of ice-cold water over Theodora's head, causing her to wake up. It didn't take long for the panic to set in before she began to wiggle frantically, with muffled screams coming through the duct tape.

Kareem knelt down, reaching for her mouth. "I'm going to remove the tape. Don't scream. Nobody will hear you and quite honestly, it'll give me a migraine." He snatched the tape from her mouth, and going against his request, she screamed at the top of her lungs.

"Help me! Somebody! Please!"

Kareem huffed, and snapped his finger at the henchmen, who came over, ramming his right foot into the side of Theodora's head. Her vision became blurry, the pain from the kick was unbearable.

"I told you not to scream, didn't I?" Kareem laughed, and the other council members joined in as Theodora cried from the pain. "We know you are an acquaintance of Jackson. The purebred that helps feys. We know all about his little adventures. Well, Jackson is a wanted man, and we know that he's seeking asylum." Kareem ran his fingers through Theodora's blonde hair. "Guess who was number one on his little list? You."

"I don't know where he is! I swear!" Theodora pleaded, her face soaked from her tears.

"Has he contacted you at all?" Kareem asked in a demanding voice.

"No. I haven't seen or heard from Jackson in years. Not since he helped me."

"You're lying! Where is he?" Kareem screamed at her.

"I'm not lying I swear! Please! I don't know where he is! I don't know!" Theodora cried as her life hung in the hands of the council.

"She's useless. Let's move on." Suggested Lester. Kareem knew there was a chance that she was telling the truth. But he wasn't about to let her get off easy.

"I'm going to ask you one more time young lady. You want to live, right?" Kareem fiddled with her blonde hair again. She sobbed on the cold, wet ground. She didn't know how else she could convince them that she didn't know anything. "Do you know where he is?" Kareem asked again.

"I don't know." Theodora said with a sunken voice. Kareem pressed his lips, looking at his brothers. There was no use in torturing her any longer. He ran his eyes back to Theodora, caressing her blonde locks as she lay there, shivering and petrified.

"I think we're done here fellas." He got up, reaching over to grab a bag that the henchman had been holding. He pulled out a small canister of liquid. Gasoline. He proceeded to pour it all over Theodora, drenching her from head to toe. She coughed and gaged, her eyes expanding with terror when she realized what it was.

"No! Please! I told you I didn't know anything!" She begged for her life as Kareem pulled a packet of matches from his pocket. He peered into her with hell in his eyes. A look so demonic as her terror filled him with pleasure.

"You didn't think we'd let you live, did you?" The sides of his mouth raised, forming a disturbing grin.

"You feys are a poison that has coursed through the veins of our community for far too long. We must purify our society once and for all." He pulled a single matchstick, igniting a flame as he ran the tip against the strip. He tossed the matchstick onto Theodora, watching as she wailed out in agony as the flames engulfed her.

"Let's go. Leave her." Kareem and the rest of the men turned to head out the woods and back to the car. The flames increased behind them, leaving behind nothing but Theodora's burning flesh. Kareem pulled a folded piece of paper from the inside of his jacket, unfolding it as they walked. "Let's see whose next."

CHAPTER 8

It was the morning before the full moon, and Christmas eve. It had been almost a month since Jax and River arrived at Will's house, and with no sign of the council on their tails things were beginning to feel almost normal again. They went out only during the day, two at a time. Using traps and snares that Will put together to catch their meals.

River would usually stay behind, watching the cameras with the walkie-talkie in hand as the other two set out to collect whatever the traps caught. Most of the time, they caught Jack rabbits that roamed around the land all hours of the day. Sometimes they caught racoons, which weren't as tasty, but kept them fed. Catching a deer was rare, unless they went out to hunt for them. But that required more patience and time out in the open, which would put them at risk.

When they weren't out collecting traps, they stayed inside the bunker trying to keep themselves busy. Reading, watching tv from the vintage 12-inch box that Will had hooked up in the other room. He had two other identical tv's in his room, which ran footage from the cameras that he had set up in the front of the house, and in the back. Will was quite the engineer, with various clever ways to keep the house guarded, even while they slept.

The house originally belonged to Will's uncle, who was a doomsday prepper which explained the bunkers. When he died, the home was left abandoned, and ended up becoming a safe haven for Will. He left his hometown of Marion five months after his attack, right after he met Jax. Will took what Jax taught him, combined with his own resourcefulness and made a life for himself in Bertram. Secluded, alone, and safe from the council.

River and Will stood on the porch, bundled up in their thick winter coats. Laughing and conversing about pop culture from the early 2000's. "I can't believe you missed the entire last season of The Wire! You missed out, the last episode was pretty good!" River nudged Will with her elbow.

"I lost interest after season three. It just lost its spark." Said Will, with one hand in his pocket, and the other holding a cigarette.

"What? You're crazy! That was my show! You suck." River teased, grinning at him playfully. Jax came outside carrying two empty garbage bags, catching them in the middle of their conversation.

"What did I miss?" He asked, looking at both River and Will.

"Just chatting. We all set?" Will asked, tossing his cigarette butt on the ground and smashing it out with his foot.

"Yeah." Jax handed Will one of the garbage bags. He turned to River. "We'll be back in an hour. You know the drill."

"Actually…" River bit her bottom lip, then turned to look at Will, then back at Jax. "I want to go out this time. With Will. You should stay here and relax. You've done so much already."

Jax's eyebrows raised. River's request was unexpected. "Are you sure?" He asked, sounding unconvinced.

"We'll be fine. Don't worry." Will reassured him. River moved in closer to Jax. Placing her soft gloves on his cold, red cheekbones, she leaned upwards and planted a kiss on his lips.

"I'll be fine." She smiled, and grabbed the trash bag from his hands. She proceeded to follow Will away from the house, trudging through the snow to collect the previous night's prey.

Will led her a half mile away, where the trees grew taller and the woods began to deepen. She hadn't gone this far out, and was surprised at how much land Will's uncle owned. Will led her towards one of his bear traps, that had a dead, bloody Jack Rabbit confined between its claws. River stared at the dead rabbit, almost feeling sorry for the poor animal. Will pulled the bear trap up by its chain, with the rabbit's nearly severed head swinging side to side.

"They're just like us." River uttered to Will through chattering teeth, as he tossed the trap into the plastic bag.

"Huh?" Will replied, not really paying attention.

"These animals. They were just minding their business, and out of nowhere, their lives were taken from them. Just like us." River stood there with her shoes buried in snow. Small flurries of snowflakes landed on her nose as she looked up at the overcast sky.

"Well, being near the bottom of the food chain sucks. But if they don't die, we don't eat." Will gave her a lighthearted smirk. River walked a few feet to remove a small pile of snow from a tree stump, before sitting down. Will looked at her, confused.

"What are you doing?" He asked, shifting his weight from one foot to another. "We don't have time to take breaks." River focused on the snow beneath her.

"Do you remember your first kill?" She asked, still not looking up.

Her question caught Will off guard, as he looked vacantly at River with no response. "Well, I know feys don't typically remember anything when we've turned. But did you ever find out who they were?" She looked up at him, blowing cold air from between her lips. Will walked over to where she was sitting, gesturing for her to scoot over so he could squat down next to her on the stump. He placed the trash bag on the ground between his legs.

"I don't know who my first kill was. I could smell the blood, but when I watched the news for the next few days after I turned, I didn't see anything about a dead body being found. I figured it was probably a drifter. Someone that didn't have a family looking for them." Will pulled off his hood, allowing his dreads to fall over his shoulders. "How about you?" He turned to River, waiting to hear her story.

"I killed my rapist." River was surprised at how smoothly the sentence rolled off of her tongue. This was her first time talking about the rape to anyone other than Tatiana and Tasha.

"Woah." Will's eyebrows raised, taken aback by her confession. "I'm sorry that happened to you. I can't even imagine how it must've felt after you killed him. Good, I hope."

"Actually, no. Not at first. I was horrified when I realized what I had done. That I had killed somebody. A person."

"You killed a disgusting piece of shit. Not a person." Will placed his arm around her, in an attempt to console her. River accepted his embrace, leaning her head into his side.

"Jax doesn't even know. He knows I killed Marco, but he doesn't know that Marco raped me." River began to feel the guilt of keeping this secret from him. "I don't know why I haven't told him yet. I want to… I just…" River couldn't even put her feelings into words.

"You don't have to tell anyone anything if you don't want to. You don't owe anyone your trauma. Not even your boyfriend." River appreciated him saying that, but it still didn't take away her issue of keeping it from Jax. She had just shared the most traumatic experience of her young life with this man sitting next to her. She knew she owed the guy who loved her the same trust.

"He told me he loved me. The night we got away. The first time I ever heard him say it." River thought back to that night in the rain. How Jax held her and promised her that his commitment was unfeigned.

"Do you love him, River?" Will asked.

River hesitated. This was the first time her love for Jax had ever been questioned. "I care about him more than anything. I really do. But considering the only other people I ever cared about are dead, I guess that's not saying much, huh?" She chuckled faintly. "Love is, complicated. But if you truly love him, your heart will tell you when the time is right." Will hugged her tightly with his left arm still draped around her. Will was like the big brother she never had. Having Will in her life was her first time platonically bonding with a male who wasn't her father. She appreciated his existence, at a time when she needed support the most.

"Thanks Will." She peered up at him, giving him a warm smile and getting one in return.

"Don't mention it. Now let's hurry up and finish with these traps, my ass is freezing." They both laughed, standing back on their feet to continue rounding up their catching for the day.

ꝏꝏꝏ

The sky grew dark as the sun was beginning to set. Will had already filled River in on his prep procedure for the full moon. Whenever he caught a deer, he kept the carcasses frozen in a deep freezer in the basement. He kept them specifically for the full moon.

One of the most vital tips for turning that Jax shared with the feys he encountered, was the "ball and chain" method. The "ball and chain" method is a trick where shifters attach a dead animal, or any huge chunk of raw meat to a hook. This hook is attached to a chain that they clamp around their leg. It keeps the beast distracted, like a dog chasing its tail. Eight pounds would usually do the trick, and Will kept more than that on hand.

Will, River and Jax made their way outside as the freezing temps crept down into the 20's. Will and River had to take extra precautions, to avoid hypothermia when shifting back into their human form. The closer they stayed to the house, the safer it would be for them at dawn. Will gathered his things on the porch, slowly undressing before the sun could set. He took off his coat, lifting his sweater over his head. His dark, muscular abs flexed from the pinching cold air. River turned her head, trying not to look. But snuck a glance or two out of the corner of her eye.

"Distracted?" Jax asked jokingly, catching her glances at Will.

"I just want to get this night over with." She replied, shivering while she stood in the snow with her arms folded.

"Same." Will cosigned from the porch with a less than enthusiastic grin. Jax led River to the side of the house, so she could undress with privacy. As they removed their shoes, coats and clothes, the cold stung River's skin like a thousand sharp little knives poking at her. She could feel her toes going numb, as she wished the sun would hurry up and set so she could get some relief from the agonizing cold. Even if it was just more pain.

"Can I ask you something?" asked Jax, bending in front of her, fully nude as he attached the chains to their legs.

"Go ahead." She said, clenching her jaw, trying to distract herself as she waited.

"Do you love me?"

River gave him a perplexed look. Suddenly, the discomfort from the cold drifted to the back of her mind. This abrupt question from him had her full attention. "Why are you asking me this? Now, when I'm cold, naked and miserable?" His sudden need for validation at a time like this was rather annoying, and uncalled for.

"I was just thinking about that night. When I told you I loved you. You never said it back. Just thought I'd ask." He looked into her eyes, hoping she'd answer.

"Jax, I care about you. You know that." She pinched the bridge of her nose, trying to gather her thoughts that were overwhelming her. "The only people I've ever loved were my parents and my aunt. After losing Tasha, it's just been hard for me."

The moment between them grew awkward, as River tried to find the words to express how she felt about this boy standing in front of her. Who put his life on the line for her, took her virginity and opened her heart in ways that she had never experienced before. She didn't understand why it was so hard to spit it out. "Jax... I..." A sharp pain shot through her abdomen, and River felt herself getting dizzy as she stumbled backwards.

"River! Try to relax your mind." Jax held on to her as the full moon beamed into the night's sky above them and the beast made its way through. River tried to focus as Will's screams echoed from the front of the house. But this feeling was different. River hadn't experienced this dizziness and lightheadedness before.

"I don't feel good Jax!" The pain in River's abdomen intensified as her bones began to shift underneath her skin. Another full moon, another cursed night. The beast was awakening.

Chapter 9

River could feel the warmth of the heater flow through her. The tips of her toes were still hard, as the heat worked its way gradually down to her feet. Jax sat on the floor next to the mattress, stroking her hair away from her face. He wrapped one of her tight curls around his index finger, bouncing it around while he watched the fuzzy reception of a Latin game show on the small tv. River squeezed her eyes together as the dizziness from the night before still lingered.

"How are you feeling" Jax asked. "Hopefully the tea helps with the vomiting." River had been feeling sick ever since she shifted back that morning. Nausea, dizziness, excessive sweating. She figured that it was probably just the flu. He handed her the hot cup. She sat up again, taking sip from the cup.

"I feel a little better. How's Will?' She asked.

"He's fine. He went out to call his mom. He wanted to wish her a Merry Christmas and let her know that he's okay. He should be back within the hour."

"Christmas. I almost forgot." River's lips formed a tight-lipped smile as she took a few more sips from her cup. "Merry Christmas Jax."

His face beamed with delight, as he reached into his pants pocket and retrieved a small white box. "Hank never let us celebrate holidays growing up. But I wanted this day to be special for you, in spite of everything that we've been through these past few months. Merry Christmas River."

He placed the box on her lap, as she sat there, eyes wide in admiration of his kindness. She sat the cup down on the floor beside them, opening the box that revealed an aqua blue hair pin. It was in the shape of a hibiscus flower, and was one of the most precious things she had ever seen. She grinned from ear to ear.

"I love it." She smiled. "When did you get this? How?"

"When I went out with Will to pick up emergency supplies at the general store a few days ago. I saw it on a souvenir display at the counter. I figured you would like it."

"Thank you." She picked up the hairpin, pushing back her puffed curls with one hand and clipping it onto the left side, by her ear. "I'm so grateful for you Jax, I really am." She turned to Jax, caressing the sides of his course chin with her fingertips. His beard was growing out, amplifying his gorgeous face.

She reached down to grab his hand, moving her fingers in between his. The love from his touch emitted through his warm palms. He leaned his face into hers, his soft lips brushing against her mouth as he kissed her.

"I don't want to put any pressure on you to say things you aren't ready to say. I just want you to know that it won't ever change how I feel about you." He hugged her, his left arm reached around her neck as he left gentle kisses on her face. She wrapped her arms around him, as they shared this priceless moment.

∞∞∞

Will stood huddled up at the payphone right outside the general store, his warm breath fogging up the glass window as he waited for his mother to answer. "Merry Christmas, Carol speaking."

Getting to hear his mother's pleasant voice again made him smile. "Hi mom. Merry Christmas."

"William! Wonderful to hear from you. I miss you! Hope all is well dear." She expressed joyfully.

"I'm fine mom. How are you doing?"

"Things are good. I did get some visitors a few days ago. Strange men, but nice."

Will's heart dropped. His mother never got visitors, especially not anyone that his mother didn't know. "Visitors?" He asked, a chill went down his spine.

"Yes dear. Nice men. They asked about you. They seemed worried."

He clenched his teeth, praying silently that this didn't mean what he thought it meant. "Mom… what did they say?" His heart started pounding.

"Not much, I guess. They were looking through my things, but I didn't mind. They were very polite. Does this mean you'll be coming home soon William?"

He could hear the hopefulness in her voice, followed by the sadness from missing her son. His mother had suffered a stroke seven years ago, which left her slightly mentally impaired. As old age caught up to the fragile woman, her judgement wasn't the best, which is why Will refrained from giving her any details about where he was.

"They said if I told them what I knew, that they would bring you home to me. We could make our favorite peach cobbler for the holidays like we used to! Oh that would be wonderful, wouldn't it William?" Her voice was full of excitement, thrilled by the idea of her son finally coming home. Will's heart nearly fell through his chest. *Fuck.* He rubbed his temples aggressively, breathing heavily.

"Mom… please. What did you tell them exactly?" He asked slowly, so she could comprehend his question.

"Well, I said that I didn't know where you were, but I told them that you call on holidays and birthdays only. Then they started to scroll my caller ID. They left shortly after." Will dropped the phone, enraged, burying his face into his gloves. He could hear his mother's faint voice calling for him from the other end as the phone dangled below him. He picked the phone up and placed it against his ear again.

"Mom, I've gotta go. Lock your doors and don't answer the door for anyone except the nurse, okay? I love you. Bye mom."

"I love you too William. Are you coming home soon?" She asked one last time.

He let out a huge sigh, wishing the call didn't have to end like this. "I'll be home soon. Merry Christmas mom." He hung up the phone and ran quickly back to his pick-up truck. He eyeballed his surroundings, seeing nothing but white snow and townsfolk going on about their day. Too many thoughts raced through his mind. At this point, the details didn't matter. He needed to get back to the house to warn Jax and River. Their time was up. The council was coming.

Chapter 10

Jax tossed the walkie-talkie back and forth in his hands, as he watched the footage of the front of the house. He heard Will's voice come through the receiver, but cut out immediately. Jax called through to him, checking in to make sure everything was alright.

"Will, you there?" He waited for an answer. Will didn't respond, so he called through again. "Will. Just checking to make sure everything is all good on your end. You good buddy?" Jax waited patiently again for an answer, his stomach turning as he got nervous. Still, the other end was quiet. Will, Jax and River had a system set in place to ensure the safety of each other, in the event that something would happen to one of them. If either of them went out to hunt, gather traps or drive out to pick up emergency supplies, they would have to be back within the hour. Occasionally checking in with each other via walkie-talkie. In the case of an emergency, the worst-case scenario of being discovered by the council, the house would go into lockdown.

Will had guns and ammunition stocked inside the bunker. He made sure that he would always be ready to defend himself if it ever became necessary. Jax hoped that this wasn't it. Just before he called out to Will one more time, a call came through. He felt a rush of relief as he waited for Will to respond.

"Hello Jackson." The voice cut out, and Jax felt his body go numb. It wasn't Will on the other end, and Jax knew that his worst fear had become their reality. His hands trembled as he slowly raised the walkie-talkie back up to his mouth.

"Where is Will?" Jax demanded, trying to mask his shaky tone.

"Will is with us. Your little game of hide and seek is over. We know where you are." Kareem's deep, grating voice sent chills through Jax's bones. He looked up at the cameras, and saw a black vehicle approaching the house. He darted out of the room, running to River who was still in bed resting.

"Turn the TV off! Turn off all of the lights!"

Jax ran towards the back of the bunker before River could get a word out. She tossed her blanket aside, jumping to her feet and following him to the back of the bunker. She saw him, grabbing two of Will's rifles, and a handgun moving frantically, and it only took seconds before River realized what was going on. She walked closer towards Jax as he stood with the leather strap of one of the rifles over his shoulder. Both hands held the other guns, the muscles in his chest were moving steadily as he tried to catch his breath. Blinking rapidly, he held out the other rifle for River.

"They're here. They have Will." He told her, grabbing her hand, forcing the rifle into her palm and draping the strap over her shoulders. He cupped her cheek with his free hand, bringing his face down to meet hers. The glint in his eyes was aligned with hers so perfectly, she could see her own reflection. He could feel her panic setting in, and she could feel his.

"I love you Jax." She admitted. She had a strong feeling that this was the last time she would ever get the chance to say it.

"I love you too." He hugged her closely, locking his arms around her tightly. "Stay behind me at all times." He said with his mouth near her ear. "We're going to hold out down here for as long as we can. Everything will be okay, just like I promised." He placed a soft kiss near her temple.

Jax received a call from the walkie-talkie. He unclipped it from his waist. "Still playing your games of hide and seek, are we?" Said Kareem from the other end. River and Jax could hear multiple footsteps moving back and forth above them. They were above them, in the basement. "We have your little friend, remember? It's best that you don't play games. If you care about his life." Kareem continued. River covered her mouth with her hands, terrified of the thought of them hurting Will.

"We can't let them hurt Will." River whispered to Jax.

"We can't give in this easily. It's what they're expecting. Will knows we're smarter than that." Jax told her. River began to pace around in circles, feeling the pressure from the council's attempt to leverage Will's life in exchange for theirs.

"We're the reason he's even up there. This is all on us. We have to help him. We owe it to him." She tried convincing Jax, but the unsettling expression on his face told her that he was not having it.

"They won't kill him. They're just playing on our emotions."

River's eyes bulged. She couldn't believe him. He was willing to let his best friend die. "Jax, you can't be serious right now. What makes you think they'll let him live if we don't go up there." River tried to avoid yelling through her whispers.

"If they kill him, they'll never find us."

"So maybe they won't kill him right away. But they'll torture him until he gives us up. You were the one who told me that these people were brutal. What kind of friends would we be if we just let them have him?" She stared at Jax, waiting for him to confirm her notion. He squatted down to the floor, with the walkie-talkie pressed against his forehead. Jax wanted to save Will, but not at the expense of risking River's life. He was torn.

"Fuck." Jax tossed the walkie-talkie on the ground, sending it flying toward River's foot. "You're running out of time Jackson." Said Kareem through the receiver.

River looked down at the walkie-talkie, she could hear a malicious laugh through the static. Will didn't deserve this, and she couldn't stand by and let him go down for their crimes. She picked up the walkie-talkie, placing it up to her mouth.

"River, what are you doing?" Jax dashed toward her, in an attempt to take it from her hands before she did something they would both regret.

"If we surrender, will you let him go?" River moved out of Jax's reach, taking control of the situation and doing what she felt was right.

"This must be River. It's unfortunate that we have to meet under these… circumstances." Kareem said through the receiver.

"Answer my question." River demanded.

"We don't want him. His life literally lies in your hands." The truth in his words hurt to the core. River knew he was right. "You don't want to kill yet another person do you, River?" Her heart dropped, Kareem was doing exactly what Jax said that he was trying to do. Playing into River's emotions, hitting her exactly where it hurt.

"River, give it to me." Jax reached out for the walkie-talkie, but River shifted her arm away.

"I'm doing what's right. For Will." She told Jax before calling out to Kareem one last time. "We're coming out. When we step outside, you let him go."

"You have my word." Kareem complied. Jax was stunned. He grabbed the walkie-talkie, tossing it to the ground and smashing it with his foot.

"Are you crazy!" Jax was furious.

"At least we have an advantage. Stop pretending like we have any real choices because you know we don't." River removed the rifle from around her shoulders, tossing it to the ground and walking over to the weapon storage area to grab a pistol. "I didn't say we had to give up without a fight."

Back outside, all four council members waited by the SUV, with Will handcuffed and, on his knees, next to one of their henchmen. His mouth was duct taped, and his face covered in bruises. The henchmen, who also suffered injuries to his face, held a .45 caliber at the back of Will's head, ready to pull the trigger at Kareem's command. They all waited, eyes focused on the front door of the house. They saw the door creak open slowly, as Jax stepped out first, his hands up in the air. An ominous smirk formed in unison across the faces of all four council members, as they took pleasure in seeing Jax and River admit defeat.

CHAPTER 11

Jax and River stepped out from behind the door cautiously. River stayed close behind Jax. Her heart dropped when she saw Will, beaten and bloody almost beyond recognition. His top lip was swollen, and the skin around his eyes were blackened from the bruises. He looked to River and Jax. The anguish in his eyes begged for them to go back.

"Oh my God, Will. What did they do to you?" River muttered, sickened by what she saw. Her hands trembled, itching to reach behind her and grab the gun she had stashed inside her jeans.

"We're here now. Let him go." Jax demanded. His was fuming from the sight of his friend's pain.

"I'm afraid I can't do that Jackson. You see, the council has gone a different moral route." Kareem took a few steps forward, with his hands behind his back. "Things have changed. The community is… purifying." He held his hands out, taking in the moist pine smells flowing from the trees.

"What are you talking about?" Jax asked Kareem. He realize he should've listened to his gut instincts to stay in the bunker.

"No, we had a deal!" River moved away from Jax, giving herself full view of them all. "We had a deal!" She shouted to Kareem reaching behind and pulling out the gun. With the muzzle pointed directly at Kareem. She looked at Will, who knew that his fate had been sealed. Although he couldn't speak, River could tell in his eyes that he was content. *Will.* She hurt for him, and the regret of giving in to the council washed over her. She allowed the council to play them all.

"Foolish girl." Kareem took a few more steps closer, giving River the perfect aim to take him out. His face didn't budge, but his eyes called her bluff. "There is no deal." He snapped his fingers, and the henchman sent a single bullet through Will's skull. His lifeless body fell forward.

"Will!" Jax screamed, reaching behind and pulling out a pistol. He fired two bullets at the henchman, hitting him twice in the chest. The henchman got one shot at Jax before falling, hitting him in the shoulder. Jax fell backwards, pressing the bullet wound with his right hand as blood spilled from it.

River became dizzy, paralyzed by the chaos that had unfolded in front of her. Her vision became foggy, as she saw Will dead, lying on the cold hard ground. Jax was saying something to her, but she couldn't understand him. His voice was drowned out by the ringing in her ears. She suddenly felt a pinch coming from the middle of her throat. She ran her fingers around the center of her neck, and felt something narrow. She yanked at it, and saw that it was a dart with a needle attached. She looked at Kareem, who was pointing a gun-like object at her. River went numb as she dropped to the ground, landing next to Jax.

∞∞∞

The sensation of ice-cold liquid sent River into a state of shock as she regained consciousness. She lay curled in the corner of the concrete floor of a cell. Her hands were handcuffed, and she couldn't see anything but the shadowy figure of a man standing over her.

"Wake up sweet pea. Might wanna enjoy the last bit of life you have left." The man laughed wickedly at River's misery, as he turned to exit the cell.

The doors closed automatically, leaving River alone in complete darkness. Her face went vacant, with her mouth slightly open and the color drained from her face. Will was gone, and Jax's whereabouts were unknown. For all she knew, he was dead already. Burned by the council, and she was next.

At the end of the hall, Jax sat in another cell. On the ground, slumped over. His shirt soaked with blood from his wounds, handcuffed and isolated. A thin metal ring was placed around his neck, that prevented purebreds from shifting while imprisoned. Jax, awoke from the serum right before they reached Chicago. He tried to fight his way out, but his efforts ended in multiple beatings from the council's henchmen. He screamed for River as he watched them carry her away, taking blow after blow to the gut. Kareem made it his business to ensure that Jax suffered as much as he possibly could before his scheduled execution. The light from outside the cell beamed in on his face as the automatic door slid open.

"It's been a while, my boy." Hank stepped inside of Jax's cell, tapping his cane against the concrete floor. Hank flicked on a small flashlight that he had brought with him, shining the light onto Jax's face. "The council's men really did a number on you."

Jax swung his face away from the light. "Hank…" He had no words. Face to face with the man he had betrayed. The man who raised him as his own and was the only father he had ever known. "Kayla… Desiree…I'm so sorry." He uttered, choking on his words as he was finally forced to face his guilt.

Hank took a few steps closer, with the light from the flashlight still aimed at Jax. "Was she worth it?" His stare penetrated as he waited for Jax to answer. Jax turned toward him with glossy eyes. He was silent. Hank's eyes filled with rage as he leaned in, inches away from Jax's face. "Answer me." He demanded.

"She's going to die. Isn't that enough for you?" Jax and Hank locked eyes, and the rage emitting from

Hank's soul, slowly transformed into something else. Heartbreak. He backed away from Jax.

"It was never supposed to end like this. You were supposed to be great." The mixture of resentment and hurt in Hank's voice was confusing to Jax. "I did everything right to prepare you. But just like your father, you throw it all away. For some cursed-blood bitch!" Jax's eyes shot at Hank when he mentioned his father. Hank's tone gave Jax the impression that he was hiding something.

"What are you talking about? Prepare me for what?" Jax asked with narrowed eyes. Hank sighed heavily, running his tongue across the roof of his mouth. After years of secrecy, the time to tell Jax the truth was finally upon him.

"Your father Silas wasn't just a purebred. He was a councilman."

Jax's eyes expanded, as his mouth hung open from the shock of what he had just been told.

"I was going to tell you the night of your birthday. That you, were a part of the council bloodline." Hank flicked off the flashlight, leaving them both in pitch blackness. “You and Kayla were supposed to be together. To breed my grandchildren who would share the bloodline and grow up to be rulers. But the apple didn’t fall far from the tree. Your father’s lust for human flesh and your mother’s weak cursed blood has soiled you.”

“Don’t you talk about my parent’s like that.” Jax’s emotions were all out of whack as he tried to process all of this.

“Your parents were fools!” Hank flicked the flashlight back on, aiming it at Jax again. “The real reason your father died, was because of your mother. I tried to warn him, but he refused to listen. All he cared about was… that woman.”

Jax stood on his feet, taking steps toward Hank with his restrained hands hanging in front of him. “What did you do to my father?”

“I didn’t do anything. I tried to help him. I loved your father like a brother. But his love for Carla trumped his loyalty to the council. She changed him. Three weeks before you were born, your father revealed that he would no longer be serving on the council. He wanted out, to be with your mother and live some delusional happy human life. But there is no such thing as out." Hank paused, letting out a faint sigh. "The following night, your father was executed."

"Liar!" Jax lunged at Hank, knocking the flashlight from his hands and sending it flying across the floor.

"It's the truth! The council killed your father because he betrayed them!" Hank seized Jax by the sides of his face, trying to calm him down. "I'm sorry I kept this from you. But it was for your own good!"

The automatic door slid open, and the henchman guarding it stepped inside. "Times up."

Hank let go of Jax, watching him stand before him with sunken eyes and riddled with emotional agony. "I'm afraid this is goodbye. May the Gods grant mercy on your soul, my son." He turned to head out of the cell, with the henchman following behind, sealing the door shut behind them.

Chapter 12

Jax sat in a slumped position in the corner of the cell, coming to terms with the bombshell that Hank dropped on him hours before. His eyes bloodshot red and glossy, as his entire life flashed before him. The truth about his parents was more emotionally devastating than he could have ever imagined. His entire life had been a lie. An elaborate cover up to hide the fact that his fate was ultimately out of his control. He shared a bloodline with the people responsible for the death of his parents. Taking his father's life, and leaving his mother with the burden of a broken heart, which led to her own death. Jax had unknowingly been following in the footsteps of his father, ending on a path of a similar fate.

He closed his eyes, picturing River's beautiful face and that warm smile that could light up the darkest room. He would've given anything in that moment to kiss her one last time. To tell her that he was sorry, for everything.

The doors of the cell slid open, a figure stood between Jax and the light from the hallway. Jax peered at the door with squinted eyes, seeing Hank walk inside the cell. He flicked on his flashlight, rushing toward Jax and bending down to grab a hold of his cuffed wrists. He pulled a small sharp pin from his pocket, shoving it inside the upper cut out of the lock. "Hank… what are you…"

"Be quiet." Hank demanded, as the cuffs opened, freeing Jax from his bind. "You don't have much time. I put a slumber juju on the guard. You get out of here as fast as you can." Jax stared, speechless with his eyebrows scrunched together. He didn't understand what was going on or why Hank was doing this. Hank grabbed Jax's shoulders aggressively. "Listen to me. I need you to focus. The girl, she's at the end of the hall in cell nine. The code is 6547."

Hank's mention of River heightened Jax's attention, causing him to become alert of the situation. Hank was setting him free, and he had to find River. Jax stood up, followed by Hank as they faced each other with their eyes centered on one another. Jax fixed his lips to speak, but couldn't find the words to say. "Just go." Hank uttered, handing Jax a .44 revolver. Jax made his way outside of the cell, closing the door behind him leaving Hank inside.

River. Jax scanned the hallway with his eyes, following the numbers as he urgently paced toward cell number nine. He ran his fingers across the keypad, which had dots instead of numbers. He gathered his focus and replayed the numbers Hank gave him in his head. *6547...6547...* He pressed the dots according with the right number sequence and the door to River's cell slid open. His heart thumped rapidly as he laid eyes on her weak, indisposed body.

He ran to her, kneeling to lift her up. "River, baby. Come on, we've got to get out of here." He wrapped his arms underneath her sternum, lifting her from the floor. River moaned faintly, trying to stand on her feet as she realized that it was Jax. Dizzy and disoriented, she grasped his shirt.

"Jax, I thought you were dead." Her voice was sparse, but seeing Jax alive, and ready to get her out of that bleak, dark hole lifted her spirits.

"I'm not dead, and we're not going to die." He pulled her towards the door, as she dragged her feet struggling to keep up. They headed toward an automatic door that opened to reveal another hallway.

"How do we get out?" River questioned, panicking as every second passed.

"I don't know, but I'll kill anyone in our way until we make it out."

They came to an elevator on the left side, in the center of the long hallway. Jax knew the cells were located somewhere underground, underneath headquarters. The only logical way to go, was up. He pressed the up button with the palm of his hand as he held the gun between his fingers. The elevator doors opened, and they ran inside. There were six buttons, and Jax had no idea which one led to an exit, but they didn't have time to stand around figuring it out. He pressed the fourth button, hoping that it balanced out their chances of finding a way out. They stood inside the elevator, holding each other closely as they went up to floor number four. The elevator stopped, and the doors opened, revealing another hallway, but this one was smaller than the ones below. A large henchman in a black suit came walking from behind a doorway, caught off guard by the sight of Jax and River.

Jax aimed the revolver at the man's forehead, sending a bullet directly into his skull. The man dropped to the floor, sending a loud thud echoing through the hall. Jax led River past the dead man, stepping over him and continuing through the area in their desperate search for an exit. The sounds from the gunshot must have alerted the other henchmen, as three more men came running in their direction.

Jax had the gun aimed, shooting off multiple rounds and hitting two of the men in the head. One of the bullets missed, and the other hit the third henchman in the chest. Jax missed his heart, but the wound brought him to a halt, giving Jax and River time to check the nearby doors. They tried three doors before they came across one that was unlocked. Jax opened the door, leading them both inside.

The room was dark, and a large black desk and two chairs sat inside. Jax ran over to the desk, tossing the chairs out of the way and pushing the desk over to block the door. River stood by him, using what minimal strength she had to help him get the desk up against the door. The loud kicks from the henchman trying to kick the door down sent vibrations through the desk. Alarm sounds rang through the air, and they knew that their time was running out.

River began to sweat, her mind racing at the thought of the man bursting through the door and killing them both. River searched the room, trying to find something to defend them with once Jax's bullets ran out. She noticed a black shade hanging from the wall. She ran her hands around it, causing it to fly up and reveal a large, circular tinted window.

"Jax! Look!" He turned to see what she found, and his eyes lit up at the sight of the window. He ran over to her, peering through the glass to get a look at their surroundings.

"We have to jump. We can't be that far up." Jax suggested as the bangs coming from outside got louder. River looked at him with enlarged eyes. As much as she hated the idea of jumping from a window that had to be at least three stories high, she knew they had no other options.

Jax ran to grab one of the chairs, bringing it back to the window and swinging it once against the glass. The glass cracked, as he swung it once more causing the glass to finally shatter. He tossed the chair away, grabbing a hold of River as they stood by the large opening.

"Whatever you do, don't let go."

He plunged out of the window sideways, just when the henchman had finally made his way through the door, pushing the large desk out of his way to get to them. The adrenaline rushed through River like a drug being shot through her veins as they fell from the window.

The wind filled her eardrums and the rain pricked her face as they fell through the air, landing on the cold, muddy ground beneath them. Jax landed on his back, breaking River's fall as she clung to his torso. River felt the impact of their landing in her left arm and leg as they hit the ground, sending a sharp pain through her abdomen. Purebred shifter's bones were more durable than the average human, giving Jax the advantage of taking most of the painful impact so they both could survive the fall. River looked up, and could see the man looking down on them from the window above. They may have made it out, but she knew they had to keep running. Jax came to his feet, helping River up to make sure she was alright.

"Are you hurt? I'm sorry we had to do that." He examined her arms for signs of broken bones.

"I'm hurt, but I can manage. Let's just keep going." She limped away, holding her stomach as they headed for the woods that surrounded the building.

CHAPTER 13

They trudged through the mud and freezing rain, as heavy branches from the tall oak trees towered above them. trying to get as far away from headquarters as they possibly could. River tried not to think about what would happen if they got caught. All she could focus on was getting away for good this time. Going someplace where they could never be found, by anyone or anything ever again. Jax came to a halt, screaming and grasping the metal collar that was still around his neck. The collar emitted an electric shock that left him in excruciating pain, as he dropped to the ground, convulsing in agony."

"Jax! What's wrong!" She fell to her knees, trying to figure out how to stop the pain. She touched the collar, immediately jerking her cuffed hands away when the shock pierced her skin. Jax continued to flail around in pain, as River heard footsteps coming in their direction.

"Go! Leave me!" He mumbled through clenched teeth.

"No! I'm not leaving you!" River sat at his side, her knees buried in the mud. She wasn't going to abandon him, even if it meant giving up her last chance at freedom. "I'm staying right here." She grabbed his hand, holding it tightly as the henchmen closed in on them.

Kareem came from behind the group of men, walking up to River and Jax with a small three inch remote in his hands. His thumb was pressed down on the button in the middle.

"I have to admit, I really do admire you two. You really know how to keep us on our toes."

Kareem raised his thumb from the button, and the electric shock coming from the collar had ceased. Jax let out a loud sigh of relief as the pain concluded. One of the henchman took hold of River, dragging her away from Jax as she screamed out for him, punching the man with both bound fists as he picked her up, flinging her over his shoulder.

"Why don't you just kill us now?" River yelled. "Just get it over with already!"

The sides of his face raised, revealing a sinister smile. "Because watching you burn is worth it." He kicked Jax in his right rib, not once but twice. Jax screeched out in pain, curling up into a ball as Kareen proceeded to kick him again. "Get the grounds ready, and get that foul traitor Hank as well. We finish this today." The henchmen picked Jax up from the ground, dragging him back to headquarters.

∞∞∞

The wide patch of dirt formed a circular ritual-like setting in the center of the woods, with a metal U-shaped frame standing ten feet from the ground. In the middle of the frame, a hook dangled. River, Jax, and Hank, sat separated at the edge of the circle with their mouth taped, and bound by their ankles and wrists as they awaited their executions. River and Jax had their eyes glued on one another, A single tear slid down Jax's right cheek, his chest pumping from his heavy breathing. River didn't cry. Her body had no more tears to spare. This was the end of her life, and somehow, she was content. But her heart still broke for Jax. She knew his tear wasn't for himself, but for her. Neither of them wanted the other to die, and that was the real tragedy.

"The girl goes first. Then Jackson, then Hank. I want them to suffer, watching the ones they love burn before they meet their deaths."

Kareem walked with his hands behind his back, followed by Lester, Jon and Edward toward the middle of the circle. Over a dozen shifters, mostly those who worked at Headquarters gathered around to watch the execution. Normally, elders from all over the region would attend as witnesses, but the last-minute decision to move things up caused a change of plans. "Grab her." Kareem ordered to the henchmen. They lifted up River, dragging her toward the center of the circle. Jax's muffled screams resonated through the area, as he watched in horror while they hung River by her ankles in the middle of the frame. She began to feel sick, clenching her eyes closed as vertigo began to set in.

"River Lewis. Responsible for the deaths of Kayla Cooper, Desiree Cooper, and Leon Cooper. We hereby sentence you to death." Jon spoke with no remorse as he waved for the henchman to bring him the lit torch. A second henchman doused River with gasoline, as she gagged from the horrid stench. Jax's muffled screams got louder. Jon held the lit torch as he stood two feet away from River. Her heart pounded, and her stomach twisted into knots as she closed her eyes, forced to accept death's embrace.

"Stop!" A female voice chimed in from outside the circle. Jon halted, with the torch still in hand, as he and everyone else looked around with confusion. A tall woman with short blonde hair, slicked backwards behind her ears appeared from behind a crowd on the left. Her bold green eyes sent a shock through Jon as she headed toward the center of the circle.

"Martina?" Jon whispered under his breath as she marched toward him.

"Put that torch down, or we'll kill you where you stand." She glared at him, as twelve more people arrived from outside the circle. The crowd gasped, looking at each other and whispering as the council members from Regions One and Three accompanied by their henchmen appeared before them to interrupt the execution. "Now." She reiterated, as Jon slowly handed the torch to a henchman, who doused the flame out with water.

"What is the meaning of this?" Kareem's eyes expanded with anger, veins emerging from his forehead as he confronted Martina, a council member from Region One. "Why are you here?" They stood face to face, both nearly identical in height.

"You didn't think you could get away with your little killing spree, did you?" Martina said to him. her lips formed a small smirk as she observed his expression. Hank didn't budge, he stood his ground, unintimidated by Martina or her crew.

"What goes on in my region is out of your jurisdiction. Go back to California, this is none of your business."

"I don't think so." Another woman approached them, shorter than Martina with a faded haircut and dark skin. Pamela, from Region Three. "The unauthorized murder of shifters from any region is all of our business. You and your council are being legally reprimanded for your actions."

"Reprimanded for taking the necessary steps to catch fugitives? This is nonsense!" Kareem was furious.

"You went against strict protocol to feed your own half-baked agenda. As a member of the council, and an elite member of the community, I expected better from you. But I can't say I'm surprised." Pamela gave him a sarcastic grin. "Release these prisoners. We'll be taking it from here." Pamela snapped her fingers, and one of the henchmen from her region approached River, removing the tape from her mouth and cutting her down from the frame. The other henchmen grabbed Hank and Jax, removing the tape from their mouths. The council members of Regions One and Three surrounded Hank and his men, holding the same metal collars that Kareem had used for Jax.

"Kareem, Jon, Lester, and Edward. Council men of Region Two, you have herby been stripped of your titles of authority. You will be taken prisoner at Headquarters in Region Three until your trial. But I wouldn't get your hopes up in a ruling in your favor." Martina winked at Kareem, watching in satisfaction as the Henchmen placed the metal collar around his neck.

"You've gone soft. All of you. It's pathetic. I did what needed to be done. You should be kissing my feet." Kareem said angrily through clenched teeth.

Martina moved in closer, the tip of her nose pressing against Kareem's. "The only pathetic one is you. Taking the lives of the innocent and putting shame on the entire community. You deserve to burn. You and your retched lackies." She backed away from him, as the rest of the Region Two council and their henchmen were given collars.

"You are being charged in the death of Theodora Banks…" Jax's heart sank as he listened to Pamela read off the names of the murdered shifters. The shifters he had befriended, that trusted him. All dead because of Kareem.

"You son of a bitch! You killed them all!" Jax began to charge at Kareem, but the henchmen held him back before he could get to him.

"Take the prisoners back to the van. We're done here." Martina ordered for everyone to clear the scene, as they prepared to head back to the Headquarters building.

CHAPTER 14

River, Jax and Hank were all led to separate vans to be transported back to headquarters. were all put in different vehicles. River sat in one of the vans with Martina and Pamela sitting across from her. The two women stared at her, with blank faces that made her uncomfortable. They were only a few minutes away from the building, so thankfully for River, the uncomfortable feeling wouldn't last long.

"River, is it? You're a beautiful young lady." Pamela complimented, with a blanketed smile. River didn't respond. She didn't know what would happen following her cancelled execution. The mention of a trial gave River an ounce of hope, but even the opportunity to plead her case wouldn't guarantee her freedom. She was still responsible for killing two shifters, not including Desiree, who was killed by Tasha. She wondered if the council would still hold her responsible for Desiree's death.

"What happens now?" River asked.

“The leaders of Region Two will be put on trial in Texas, where their fates will be determined. However, you, Jackson and Hank will be dealt with here. If found guilty, you will face either imprisonment or execution.” Marina’s words killed the small amount of hope that River had left. There was no way they would let her go. Not for all three murders. “But, unlike Kareem and his men, we believe that every shifter should be able to defend themselves and given a second chance. Purebreds and feys alike.”

“We believe in growth, and progressing as the times change. The methods of punishment used by our community have become inhumane and outdated.” Pamela chimed in. “Unfortunately, some leaders have a hard time adjusting to change. But they are in the minority, and won’t be an issue for long.” Martina and Pamela gave each other gratifying glances, and River knew they were referring to Kareem and his men.

“What about Jax? He only killed to protect me. He never meant to hurt anybody.” Said River.

"We're aware of that. But as you may know, Jackson is… special." Said Martina.

River squinted her eyes at them. "What is that supposed to mean?" The two women looked to her with pity, realizing that she had most likely been unaware of Jax's family past.

"Jackson's father was a member of the council. Which makes him next in line for leadership in Region Two."

"What?" River was dumbfounded, as she sat with her mouth hanging open. It was as if her entire relationship with Jax had suddenly come crashing down. Her heart wanted to believe that there was no way he could've known about this. He would never keep a secret like that from her. Especially considering everything they had been through. *Or could he?*

"We're here." Said Martina as they arrived at headquarters. River was escorted out of the van, with her hands still bound with the rope. She could see Jax and Hank being escorted out of one of the other vans to her right, but everyone was moving so fast that her and Jax couldn't get more than a few seconds glance at each other. But she could hear him calling for her as he was forced inside the building.

Once they walked through the large double doors, everyone made their way to the sixth floor, where the main conference room was located. What only took a few minutes, felt like a lifetime as River nervously anticipated her trial. The members of the council from Regions One and Three all sat in seats that surrounded the onyx marble table. Kareem, and the other members of his council, were huddled in a corner in their metal collars, surrounded by henchmen guards.

"Jackson, please come before the council." Pamela called to him. Jax gazed around the room as all eyes were on him. He slowly approached the front of the room, standing before all eight members. Pamela stood up from her seat. "Jackson Kinnard, responsible for the deaths of four servicemen, and harboring a fugitive. How do you plead?" Silence filled the air, as Jax hesitated before he could give an answer. He looked at River, who stood at the edge of the room, staring at him with a solemn face. She turned her head away, breaking eye contact. She didn't want his feelings for her getting in the way of him making the right choice for himself.

"Not guilty." He answered. The council members all looked at each other, more impressed than surprised by his plea of innocence.

"Why do you feel you are innocent?" Pamela questioned.

"I did what I had to do to save myself. My friend Will was killed. The man who killed him deserved to die." Martina raised her left eyebrow, grazing her chin with her right index finger. "As for the other men I killed, it was either us or them. Like I said, I did what I had to do, and I don't regret any decision I've made that have kept me and River alive."

Pamela looked to all the council members for their consideration before the vote commenced. One of the other council members gave her a subtle nod, as she turned back to face Jax, prepared to declare his fate.

"All those on the council that vote in favor for his innocence, raise your hands now."

Martina's hand went up first, followed by four others, one of them including Pamela. River let out a loud sigh of relief from the back of the room, holding her palms together with her head raised to the ceiling. Jax would be free, and for a moment, she no longer cared what her own fate would be. For once, someone she loved wouldn't suffer because of her, and that's all that mattered. But Jax didn't seem so happy about their decision. His main concern was River, and if he could get her out of this. One of the henchmen approached Jax to cut his hands free and remove his collar.

"This is absurd!" Kareem blurted out. "You idiots don't deserve to serve on the council!" An electric shock sent Kareem to his knees, convulsing in pain as Martina held the device that controlled his metal collar. Her thumb pressed against the button with force, as she took pleasure in watching him suffer.

"Speak again, and I'll turn your insides into mush." She threatened through gritted teeth before letting go of the button. Kareem tried to catch his breath, squirming on the floor like a feeble child.

Pamela continued with the trial proceedings. "Up next, River Lewis."

Chapter 15

River made her way toward the front of the room, taking slow paces forward and keeping her head down as she passed by the council's table. She stood front and center, feeling like she was already being executed before a verdict had been given. "River Lewis, responsible for the deaths of Kayla Cooper, and Leon Cooper. How do you plead?" Asked Pamela.

River looked down at her bound wrists, which were bruising red from the tightness of the rope. She looked back up at the council, and could see Jax peering at her from the corner of her eye. She inhaled slowly, taking in the cold air from the room. "Guilty."

Jax's eyes shot up in disbelief. "River, you don't have to do this!"

The council members looked around at each other, surprised by River's bold plea. "Why do you believe you are guilty and should face punishment?" Pamela asked.

River thought about every aspect of her short life that brought her to this moment. Every decision she ever made that led her to this room, in front of these people. Memories of the day her parents died flashed through her mind. Watching her mother lean against the passenger door of their family car as nine-year-old River tugged at the hem of her mother's dress, begging to ride in the front seat. *Anything for my little girl.* Her mother kissed her on the cheek, and River could still feel her mother's touch from all those years ago.

"I killed Kayla. I was angry, because she murdered by best friend. That night at the party, I let my emotions get the best of me. Instead of allowing the council to punish her for her actions, I decided to take matters into my own hands. It got my aunt killed." Tears began to flow from River's eyes as she gave her emotional testimony. "She killed Desiree, but only because she was protecting me. I put her in that position, I'm responsible." River closed her eyes, and she could see her mother's face again. "I'm responsible."

Everyone in the room stood silent, as Pamela, Martina, and the rest of the council gathered their thoughts before making a final verdict. Pamela's eyes circled the table, before getting the final acknowledgement from every member. "All those on the council that vote in favor of her innocence, raise your hands now." Four members of the council raised their hands, including Pamela. That left four other members who found her guilty. River didn't know what this meant, and judging by the shock on the faces of everyone in the room, neither did they. "Well, looks like we have a tie. This is interesting." Martina said with a raised eyebrow.

"There is no tie." Jax approached the table with his hand raised. Each member of the council turned their heads in contempt. "I vote in favor of her innocence." He said.

"You can't do that." Said Martina. "Birthright or not, you haven't taken your oath to serve on the council."

"I don't need to. You've already stripped Kareem and the rest of the leaders in my region of their roles.

Region Two has no active members of the council. I'm of age, which makes my role effective immediately." The council members muttered within each other, questioning the validity of this rule that Jax had just thrown at them.

"He's right." Said Pamela. "There are currently no active members in Region Two, which makes Jackson's leadership official. His vote is valid."

Martina looked at Pamela with pursed lips, knowing her words couldn't be challenged. Martina looked back at Jax. He was even more clever than she thought. "Well I guess it stands then. River Lewis, you are free to go."

River couldn't believe it. She stood there, frozen and unsure if she was hallucinating. But the second Jax ran over to her, grabbing ahold of her arms and kissing her with every ounce of energy he had in him, she knew it was real. One of the henchmen walked up to her, interrupting their intimate moment to cut the rope from her wrists. The rope fell away, as she threw her arms around Jax, squeezing his rib cage. The entire room watched in awe as the young couple's love radiated the room.

"I'm so sorry, about everything. I just want you to know that."

Jax kissed her again, with his hands pressing the sides of her face. After all the pain, the running, the fighting, it was all over. But River didn't understand what his new role as councilman would mean for their relationship. She still wanted nothing to do with the community, but Jax had already agreed to his commitment. This didn't sit well with her.

"What about the council?" She pondered. "You're one of them now."

"None of that matters right now. We'll make it work. I promise." He caressed the edges of her mouth with his fingertips.

"Alright, that's enough." Said Martina, rolling her eyes at their adolescent romance. "We've still got work to do."

Jax and River moved away from the center, as the council prepared for Hank's trial. As Jax led River towards the back of the room, River saw a figure moving from the corner of her eye. She looked to her left, and that's when she saw him. Kareem had snatched a gun from the holster of the henchman guarding him. He aimed it in their direction, the barrel of the gun pointed directly at Jax. River's stomach dropped, as her whole world came to a standstill. She pulled herself against him, clenching the sleeves of his shirt as two bullets pierced through her. She hung from him, as blood soaked through her shirt.

"River!" Jax held on to her as her arms dropped to her sides, his hands covered in the blood gushing from her wounds. Chaos erupted in the room as two henchman tackled Kareem to the ground, disarming him before he could fire another bullet. Martina raised up from her seat, pressing down on the device that controlled Kareem's collar.

"Get him out of here! Now!" Martina demanded, running over to Jax and River. River's nearly lifeless body laid in-between his lap as he sat on the floor, his hands shivering, and his body overwhelmed with shock as he held her.

"No-no-no-no! You've gotta stay with me! River please!" He pleaded through quivering lips. He ran his blood-smeared hands over her face, brushing her hair away from her eyes. She looked him in the eyes, as her vision became glossy. Her breathing became shallow, her last words getting caught between gasping breaths.

"I'm… o-okay." She uttered as blood filled her lungs. She could hear people gathering around her, but her only focus was on Jax.

"Somebody help her! Please!" Jax begged. His eyes darted around the room waiting for someone, anyone, to do something. Hank approached Jax, kneeling down beside him and placing his hands on Jax's shoulder.

"She's gone. You have to let her go." Hank told him.

"No. I won't let her die." Jax said to Hank. He peered down at River, as she held on to her final breaths for as long as she could. "I won't let you die. You can't leave me." The tears flowed from his eyes as he cradled her, holding the side of her face with his palms. River didn't speak. She just smiled. A smile that told him, that it was okay to let go. She was ready to accept death's hand into the afterlife.

"There is a way. To save her life. But it comes at a cost." Martina told Jax as she kneeled next to him while he grieved. Jax's eyes shot up at her, wondering what exactly it was that she had up her sleeve. Whatever it was, he was more than willing to take a chance. "Only the blood of a purebred can save her life." Martina reached over to one of her henchmen, and pulled a small metallic pocket knife from his jacket. "She must drink from the flesh of the pure. But in doing so, you give up your human form forever." She unfolded the knife, exposing the sharp blade.

"Jackson, you can't possibly consider doing this." Hank protested. But Jax didn't acknowledge him. He just looked down at River, who was still breathing but losing consciousness. He knew that he was running out of time.

"Give it to me." Jax held his hand out for Martina to hand him the knife.

“Are you sure you want to do this? I must remind you, that you will be making the ultimate sacrifice.” Martina reiterated to him.

“I would sacrifice anything for her.”

Martina stood in admiration of his bravery, as she held out the knife. Jax grabbed it from her hands, holding up his left forearm, and slicing through the middle of his palm. “I love you.” He whispered as the blood seeped through his skin. Hank grabbed Jax’s arm before a drop of his blood could reach River’s lips. Jax turned to him, startled by his sudden objection. Hank grabbed the knife from Jax, turning it on himself and making a vertical cut down his forearm. He raised his arm over River’s face, allowing his blood to trickle into her mouth. Heaves of shock swept the room as everyone stood, jarred by Hank’s decision to sacrifice himself. Jax was speechless.

“Everyone I love is gone. I have no need for this body any longer.” Hank placed his hand on Jax’s face. “Live well, my son.” His skin began to retract, as his human form began to dissipate for the last time.

Within seconds, Hank's human body was gone, and the beast emerged in its place. River's eyes opened slowly, as she inhaled sharply with her chest extended. She coughed and gagged, sprinkling specs of blood onto Jax's shirt as he sat her up. Trying to catch her breath, she gazed around at everyone watching. Faces full of shock and reverence from what they had just witnessed. River turned her eyes to Jax. He used his fingers to wipe the blood from her mouth. Their brown eyes, fixed on one another.

Epilogue

Four years later...

The sun began to set over the horizon as River watched from her bedroom window, rubbing her second trimester belly. Her door creaked open, and her three-year-old daughter Hope ran inside, jumping up and down excitedly.

"Is it almost time mama? Is it?"

River leaned over to pick her up, holding little Hope on her hip. "Almost sweetie." River placed a gentle kiss on her daughters cheek. Brushing her soft curls with her hand.

"But I wanna do it now! Can I? Please mommy?" Hope begged with pouted lips.

"Did you ask your father?"

Hope dropped her head. "No." River giggled, placing another kiss on Hope's cheek. Jax stood at the door, watching them with a smile on his face. Hope jumped down from her mother's arms and ran to her father. "Daddy! Can I turn now? I don't wanna wait! Please?" She yanked at his pants leg.

"Be patient baby girl. No early shifting, you know that. Why don't you go out to the yard and get ready? Mommy and I will be out in a minute."

"M'kay!" Hope ran downstairs and out to the yard, kicking off her sandals as she twirled around in the grass, waiting for the full moon to rise.

A few days after the trial, River discovered that she was pregnant with baby Hope. After suffering through so much, and getting yet another chance at life, River and Jax were overjoyed at the news of becoming parents. After months of negotiating with the council members from the other regions, they temporarily allowed Jax to work away from Illinois. He took River back to Iowa where they moved into Will's house, fixing it up and turning it into a real home as the two prepared for the birth of their daughter.

After their trials, Kareem was sentenced to death, while Jon, Lester, and Edward all served out life sentences at headquarters in Region Three. Jon's oldest daughter, Lisa was next of age to serve on the council, turning twenty not too long after Jax. She agreed to his request to permanently reside in Iowa, where he would still serve on the council but only visit headquarters when his attendance was needed. River wasn't too keen on the idea of Jax holding leadership, but was willing to deal with it as long as she could raise their family in peace. Her new life in Bertram with Jax and their children was the epitome of everything River had always wanted. True love and peace of mind. Life was perfect.

Things in the shifter community had finally begun to change for the better. Feys in every region were now assigned a guide, who would assist them during the full moon. Jax honored the memory of his parents, Will, and his other friends by using his role to enforce change, safety, and equality within his community. His policies were reshaping an entire generation of shifters, bridging the gap between the pure and the cursed. There was still plenty of work to do, but a step forward in the right direction was always better than no progress at all.

Jax walked over to the window where River was standing, positioning his palm on her belly. She placed her hand on top of his as they felt their unborn child shuffle around inside. “I hope it’s a boy this time.” Said Jax.

“Me too.” River leaned her head against his chest, as they both gazed out of the window, and into the moonlight.

ABOUT THE AUTHOR

Born and raised in the Washington D.C. area, writing has been a passion of mine since I was young. I started writing my first book, 'My Colorblind Rainbow' in 2013. In 2017, I decided to continue writing, taking a leap of faith and following my dreams of publishing my first book which made the 'In the Margins Award Long List' for YA fiction 2018. I launched **Hardy Publications** in September of 2017, working as a freelance ghostwriter, author, and literary blogger. I also use my platform to raise awareness for different charities and non-profit organizations, donating a portion of my book royalties to help others in need.